the Cheetah girls

shop in the Name of Love

Deborah Gregory

JUMP AT THE SUN

HYPERION PAPERBACKS FOR CHILDREN

NEW YORK

Fashion credits: Photography by Charlie Pizzarello. Models: Imani Parks, Mia Lee, Brandi Stewart, Arike Rice, and Jeni Rice-Genzuk. On Imani (Dorinda): jacket and skirt, The Children's Place, mesh tank by Daang Goodman for Tripp, NYC, satin Mary Janes by Steve Madden. On Mia (Galleria): red and black pony-print coat by XOXO, red pullover by Essendi, black flat-front trousers by Daang Goodman for Tripp, NYC. On Brandi (Chanel): white leopard coat by XOXO, yellow knit top by Essendi, grey velvet snake-print pants by Daang Goodman for Tripp, NYC. On Arike (Aquanette): black faux-fur coat by XOXO, purple leopard top and skirt by to the max, purple furry hat by Kangol, orange leopard bag by Betsey Johnson. On Jeni (Anginette): dark red faux-fur coat by XOXO, cowl-neck knit top by Essendi, snake-print skirt by Betsey Johnson, red furry hat by Kangol. All gloves by LaCrasia. All hosiery by Look From London. Hair by Jeffrey Woodley. Makeup by Lanier Long. Fashion styling by Sharon Chatmon Miller.

Printed in the United States of America.

First Edition

3 5 7 9 10 8 6 4

This book is set in 12-point Palatino.

Library of Congress Catalog Card Number: 99-61154.

ISBN: 0-7868-1385-7

For my fluffy,
smoochy, barky
boo-boo Cappuccino
I wuv you.

The Cheetah Girls Credo

To earn my spots and rightful place in the world, I solemnly swear to honor and uphold the Cheetah Girls oath:

- 🐾 Cheetah Girls don't litter, they glitter. I will help my family, friends, and other Cheetah Girls whenever they need my love, support, or a *really* big hug.

- 🐾 All Cheetah Girls are created equal, but we are not alike. We come in different sizes, shapes, and colors, and hail from different cultures. I will not judge others by the color of their spots, but by their character.

☙ A true Cheetah Girl doesn't spend more time doing her hair than her homework. Hair extensions may be career extensions, but talent and skills will pay my bills.

☙ True Cheetah Girls *can* achieve without a weave—or a wiggle, jiggle, or a giggle. I promise to rely (mostly) on my brains, heart, and courage to reach my cheetah-licious potential!

☙ A brave Cheetah Girl isn't afraid to admit when she's scared. I promise to get on my knees and summon the growl power of the Cheetah Girls who came before me—including my mom, grandmoms, and the Supremes—and ask them to help me be strong.

☙ All Cheetah Girls make mistakes. I promise to admit when I'm wrong and will work to make it right. I'll also say I'm sorry, even when I don't want to.

☙ Grown-ups are not always right, but they are bigger, older, and louder. I will treat my teachers, parents, and people of authority with respect—and expect them to do the same!

🐾 True Cheetah Girls don't run with wolves or hang with hyenas. True Cheetahs pick much better friends. I will not try to get other people's approval by acting like a copycat.

🐾 To become the Cheetah Girl that only *I* can be, I promise not to follow anyone else's dreams but my own. No matter how much I quiver, shake, shiver, and quake!

🐾 Cheetah Girls were born for adventure. I promise to learn a language other than my own and travel around the world to meet my fellow Cheetah Girls.

Chapter 1

Princess Pamela does *la dopa* braids, thanks to me. When I was ten years old, I taught her how to do all the *coolio* styles—frozen Shirley Temple curls, supa dupa *flipas* that don't flop, and even unbeweavable weaves. Of course, I was too young to go to beauty school, but sometimes, *tú sabes que tú sabes*—you know what you know—as my Abuela Florita says. *Abuela* means grandma in Spanish. And my *abuela* knows what she knows, *está bien?*

Doing hair and singing are what I—Chanel Coco Cristalle Duarte Rodriguez Domingo Simmons—know best. (You don't have to worry about remembering all my names, because everyone just calls me Chanel, Chuchie, or Miss

Cuchifrito—except for my Abuela Florita, who now calls me by my Confirmation name, Cristalle, because, she says, I'm a shining star—*una estrella.*)

Now that I'm part of the Cheetah Girls—a girl group that is destined to become *muy famoso*—one day I will have lots of *dinero* to open my own hair salons. Miss Cuchifrito's Curlz—yeah, there'll be two of them, right next door to both of my dad's restaurants, so that I get to see him more.

"Chanel, you musta wear the braids bigger, like thiz, from now on. Don't you think you look so boot-i-full?" Princess Pamela coos in her sugar-cane accent. I love the way she talks. She is from Transylvania, Romania, home of Count Dracula and a thousand vampire stories. Her native language is Romanian, which is one of the romance languages—like Spanish, my second language. Now me and Bubbles, my best friend since the goo-goo ga-ga days, say "boot-i-full," exactly the way Princess Pamela does.

My mom doesn't know that Princess Pamela braids my hair. She thinks that Bubbles does it. *Qué broma*—what a joke! Bubbles (a.k.a. Galleria Garibaldi) does not have a "green

2

thumb" for hair. She knows how to write songs, and how to make things happen faster than Minute Rice—but I would look like "Baldilocks" if she did my hair, *comprende*?

I think that once you find out who Princess Pamela is, though, you'll understand why a smart *señorita* such as myself must resort to "fib-eronis" (as Bubbles calls them) just to keep *poco paz*—a little peace—in my house.

"Oooh, they do look nice bigger like this," I coo back at Princess Pamela, looking in the mirror at my longer, fatter braids and shaking them.

I'm so glad I got my hair done today. I usually wait three months, or until I have collected "fuzz balls" on my braids—whichever comes first. But this time is different. We, the Cheetah Girls, have a very important *lonchando* meeting coming up, with Mr. Jackal Johnson of Johnson Management. He was at our first show: at the Kats and Kittys Halloween bash at the world-famous Cheetah-Rama nightclub. We turned the place upside down, if I do say so myself—and we even made four hundred dollars each after expenses, *muchas gracias*!

Anyway, Mr. Johnson came backstage after,

and said he wanted to be our manager—and take us to the top! *Está bien* with me, because the top is where I belong.

Now back to the real-life Spanish soap opera that is my *vida loca*—my crazy life—and why I have to make up stories about who does my hair.

Five long years ago, when I was nine years old, my dad left my mom for Princess Pamela. I still see him every once in a while, but I miss him a lot. So does Pucci, my younger brother.

Back then, when my dad first met Princess Pamela, she had a "winky dink" tarot shop around the corner from our loft in Soho on Mercer Street. It was so small, if you blinked or winked, you missed it, get it? Back then, her name was Pasha Pavlovia, or something like that, but we just called her "the psychic lady."

My dad's name is Dodo, but he is not a dodo. His nickname is short for Darius Diego Domingo Simmons. He was only four years old when he and his sister had to get out of their beds in Havana, Cuba, and escape when Fidel Castro took over. They were sent to relatives in Jamaica, but my dad says he misses his father every day. He misses the smell of the grass, too, and more than anything else, the water. There are no beaches like the ones in Havana, my dad says.

In that way, he and Princess Pamela have a lot in common. She had to leave Romania as a child when the Communists took over there, too. They both know what it's like to lose everything you have and never see your home again. They both have that sadness in their eyes sometimes.

Princess Pamela says when she saw my dad it was "love at first bite." He came into the shop for a reading and I guess he fell under her spell. Princess Pamela is a *bruja*—a witch—who can see the future. Mom hates her, but I think she is a good witch, not a bad one.

"Let me see how it looks with the head-band!" I exclaim excitedly, and jump out of the beauty salon chair, hitting myself in the fore-head with the red crystal bead curtains that divide the psychic salon from the beauty salon in the back.

"Ouch," I wince as I separate them to go to the front. See, thanks to my dad, Princess Pamela's Psychic Palace on Spring Street is now *muy grande* and beautiful. He built the whole place with his own two hands. He also helped Pamela install her Psychic Hotline, where she gives advice over the phone.

And thanks to her nimble fingers (and me), she now has a hair salon in the back. She even changed her name to Princess Pamela—because "it is a very good name for business—Pamela rhymes with stamina. It can unleash the secret energy into the universe."

Princess Pamela also loves music with flavor—*con sabor*—reggae music, rap, salsa. Sometimes I bring her cassettes, and we dance around if there aren't any customers. She likes Princess Erika, Nefertiti, and Queen Latifah the best. "Why not the Black people here should be like royalty? They can make their own royal family," she jokes, her accent as thick as ever.

My dad also built two other stores for Princess Pamela—Princess Pamela's Pampering Palace and Princess Pamela's Pound Cake Palace—both on 210th Street and Broadway. *The New York Times* rated her pound cake "the finger-lickin' best in New York City."

I am proud of her, and I think Princess Pamela is going to be Pamela *Trumpa* one day, and take a huge bite out of the Big Apple!

"Which headband do you think I should wear, the pink one or the green one?" I yell back to her, as I pull them out of my cheetah backpack. I just got these headbands from Oophelia's catalog—my favorite un-store in the entire universe.

Pink is my favorite color. Or sometimes red is. I like them both a lot. So does Princess Pamela—her whole place is covered in red velvet. Leopard, which is a "color" the Cheetah Girls use a lot, is my third favorite.

"*Ay, Dios mío*, what time is it?" I shriek. "I've got to get home!"

Bubbles, Dorinda Rogers, and Aquanette and Anginette Walker—the other members of the Cheetah Girls—are coming over to my house at seven o'clock so we can practice table manners for our *lonchando* meeting with Mr. Johnson. It may be the most important meeting I ever have. My mom is making dinner for us, and she doesn't like it if I'm not around to help—even though she won't let me get near the kitchen when she's working in there.

See, my mom is very *dramática*. She likes to have her way all the time—and know where I am *all the time*, which is right about now, so I'd better get home.

"I have to go!" I yell to Princess Pamela, who is on the phone fighting with someone.

"No! For that money, I can order flour from the King of Romania, you *strudelhead*!" she huffs into the phone. Then she wraps herself in her flowered shawl and comes toward me, with a little blue box in her hand. "Before you run off—this is for you, dahling," she says, smiling.

My heart is pounding. It is a present from Tiffany's!

"Chanel, this will bring you good luck with your meeting, so you will get many royalties," Princess Pamela says, kissing me on my cheeks and handing me my present. "You get my joke, no?"

"Joke?" I repeat, squinching up my nose.

"When you have a record, you get the royalties. You understand now?"

"Yeah," I giggle. "Besides, maybe I am going to be royalty for real, soon, because of my mom's new boyfriend, Mr. Tycoon, right?"

"Right, dahling. And how is he?"

"He's in Paris right now, and Mom's going crazy waiting for him to get back," I say, rolling my eyes. "You should see her—she's on my case all the time."

I don't want to get into my problems with my mom in front of Princess Pamela, so I keep my mouth shut and open the box. "*Ay, Dios mío!* Real diamonds!" I cry, and hug the princess. I hold up the diamonds to the light to admire them, and then I put my beautiful little diamond studs in my ears.

"Diamonds are a Cheetah Girl's best friend!" Princess Pamela sings, in such a funny voice that I can't stop laughing. "You think I could be a Cheetah Girl, too, and be in your group, Chanel?"

I just giggle at her, wishing I could stay longer. Princess Pamela is so dope—being with her is just like being with my crew. I wish it could be like that between me and my mom, instead of things always being so tense.

"*La revedere*—I gotta go!" I kiss her on the cheek, and hug her tight.

"*La revedere*," she whispers back, saying good-bye in Romanian, and kisses me on the cheek.

When I get outside on Spring Street, it is really crowded. On the weekends, thousands of tourists and native New Yorkers come down to

Soho to shop. They will do the Road Runner over you, too, if you happen to be walking by one of the boutiques where there is a sale! One lady gets a little huffy, like Puff the Magic Dragon, when I don't walk fast enough in front of her—but that is like a breath of fresh air compared to the fire my mom is puffing down my back when I get home.

She is standing in the kitchen, with a spatula in her hand and an Yves Saint Bernard facial mask on her face. It covers her whole face except her eyes and mouth, and it is this putrid shade of yellow-green.

Cuatro yuks! She does the mask thing every Sunday afternoon. She thinks it keeps her looking young for her tycoon, and it must work, too, because he seems pretty gaga for her.

"Do you know what time it is? I'm not here to cook dinner for you and your friends, and to entertain them while you're out somewhere having fun, you understand me?"

"*Lo siento, Mamí.* I'm sorry. I know I'm late!" I exclaim.

"Why aren't you wearing a sweater?" Mom drills me.

"I'm not cold," I squeak.

"Wear a sweater anyway. And what is that on your head?" Mom waves the spatula at me, then uses it to stir the pot of Goya *frijoles* for our Dominican style *arroz con pollo* dinner.

"It's a headband. Isn't it cute?" I exclaim.

"It looks like a bra strap!"

"It's not a bra strap. It's a headband, *Mamí*."

"Well, it *looks* like you're wearing a bra strap on your head, okay? And where did you get those?" Mom asks, pointing to my diamond stud earrings.

Uh-oh. Where is Bubbles when I need her? She'd be able to come up with something. She always does.

But I'm not that quick, and anyway, this is not the time to tell a real *mentira*—a lie that will come back to haunt me like *Tales from the Crypt*. So I decide to be honest. Why should I have to lie just because Princess Pamela gave me a present? After all, she is my dad's girlfriend, so she is *la familia* to me, I think, trying to get up my courage.

"Princess Pamela gave them to me as good luck for the meeting with Mr. Johnson. Aren't they boot-i-full?" I squeak, hoping to tap into Mom's weakness for "carats."

"She did *what*!?" she screams at the top of her lungs. Her facial mask cracks in a dozen places, and her eyes are popping big-time. Suddenly, she looks like The Mummy. Even through her tight lips, her voice is loud enough to send coyotes running for the hills.

"*When* did you see her? *Cuándo?*" Mom demands, standing with one hand on her hip and the other holding the spatula straight up in the air.

"I just stopped by there on my way home," I whine.

"Don't you *ever* take anything from that *bruja* again. Do you hear me? *Me sientes?*" she screeches, squinting her eyes. The Mummy is walking toward me. I think I'm going to faint.

"And if Bubbles did your hair, how come she didn't come back with you?" my mom asks me suspiciously. "That *bruja* Pamela does your hair, doesn't she? You think I'm stupid." She pulls on one of my braids. "You try and lie to me?"

I have not seen my mom this angry since my dad left and she threw his clothes out the window into the street, and the police came because she hit a lady on the head with one of his Oxford wing-tipped shoes.

"I'm sorry, *Mami*," I cry, praying she will stop. "I won't do it again!"

"I know you won't, because I'm gonna hang you by your braids!" says The Mummy who is my mom.

I run to my room, grab the red princess phone by my bed and beep Bubbles, putting the 911 code after my phone number. Me and Bubbles have secret codes for everything. She will understand. I sure hope she gets the message, but I know she's probably already on her way here for our dinner together.

I listen to my mom clanging pots and pans in the kitchen, and I let out a big sigh. See, me and Mom fight a lot, especially now that I am a Cheetah Girl. It seems like everything I want, she's against. She does not want me to sing. She says I should get a real job—be a department store buyer or something—because if I keep chasing my dreams of being a singer, I will get my heart broken by living *la gran fantasía*—the grand fantasy. And most of all, she does not want me to see Princess Pamela.

I sit on the edge of the bed, waiting for Bubbles to call back, and I look into the sparkly eyes of my kissing-and-tongue-wagging Snuggly-Wiggly stuffed pooch. Abuela Florita gave him to me as a joke for Christmas, because I always wanted a real dog like Toto, who is Bubbles's "big brother." (Mom won't let me have a dog because she says she is allergic to them.)

Snuggy-Wiggly Pooch is sitting on my night-stand with his tongue hanging out, next to the *Book of Spells* that Princess Pamela gave me (my mom doesn't know about that either).

I sit on my frilly canopy bed and stare at all my dolls. I have twenty-seven collectible dolls. They are *muy preciosa*—very precious—and come from all over the world.

"Charo is from Venezuela and she never cries. Zingera is from Italy and she never lies. Coco is from France and she smells so sweet, *huit, huit, huit,*" I repeat to myself, like I used to do when I was little. *Huit,* which sounds like wheat, means eight in French. It's a silly rhyme, but I like it. And right now, I just want to get my mind off my misery.

When I was little, I used to lock my bedroom door, use my hairbrush as a microphone, and sing into the mirror, thinking about all the people who would love me if they could only hear me sing. That's all I ever dreamed about—me and Bubbles singing together, and Abuela Florita sitting in the first row clapping and crying joyfully into her handkerchief.

I have always felt closer to Abuela than to my mother, because she understands me. She would never try to get in the way of my dreams the way my mom does. I know Mom's just trying to protect me from the heartbreak of failure, but why can't she believe in me the way Abuela Florita does?

I can hear Abuela's voice now, telling me what a great singer I am. She says, "*Querida Cristalle, tú eres la más bonita cantora en todo el mundo.*" I know it's not true, because Chutney Dallas is the best singer in the whole world, but it makes me want to sing just for her. Why, oh why, can't my mom see me the way Abuela does?

I let out a big yawn. Suddenly, even though Bubbles hasn't called back, even though it's not even dinnertime, I cannot keep my eyes open anymore.

Chanel is so sweet, *huit, huit, huit*. . . . I think, as I fall asleep, just like a real-life mummy. . . .

Chapter 2

The sound of the doorbell wakes me up out of my deep sleep. I'm still too scared to come out of my room. I can hear my mom talking with Aqua in the hallway. Aquanette Walker is one of the "Huggy Bear" twins (that's my and Bubbles's secret nickname for them) from Houston, Texas. We met them at the Kats and Kittys Klub barbecue last summer. They were singing, swatting mosquitoes, and eating hot dogs all at the same time. We *had* to have them in our group!

My little brother, Pucci, is running down the hall to the door. "Hi, Bubbles! I'm a Cuckoo Cougar! I'm a Cuckoo Cougar! You wanna see if you can outrun me?"

So Bubbles is here, too. I crack the door open and sneak out, to see if I can get her attention without my mom seeing me, and before Pokémon-*loco* Pucci drags Bubbles into his room to floss his Japanese "Pocket Monsters."

"I know you can run faster than me, Pucci. You are 'tha man,'" Bubbles says, hugging Pucci back.

"Are you singing, Bubbles?" Pucci whines, holding Bubbles by her waist. She is like his second big sister.

"We're all singing, Pucci—we're the Cheetah Girls—me and Dorinda and Aquanette and Anginette—and Chuchie, too," Bubbles says, pointing to our crew, who have all assembled in the hallway.

Pucci looks up at Bubbles with the longest face, and asks, "Why is it only for girls? Why can't there be Cheetah Boys, too?" Leave it to Pucci to whine on a dime.

"I wanna be a Cheetah Boy!" Pucci says, yelling even louder, then hitting Bubbles in the stomach. Pucci is getting out of control. When I see my dad, I'm gonna tell him.

"That's enough, Pucci!" Mom yells. I can tell she is still mad, by the tone of her voice. My crew can tell, too, and Bubbles looks at me like, "What's going on, *girlita*?"

"Hey, *Mamacitas*," I yell at them in the hallway. I pop my eyes open real big when my mother turns her head, so my crew knows there is something going on. *Ayúdame!* Help me, my eyes are screaming.

"Go on, sit down at the table and I'll bring your dinner in." Mom sighs with her back turned. "I'm not eating now because I'm expecting a call from Paree."

She means Paris, of course. These days, Mom uses her new French accent "at the drop of a *croissant*," as Bubbles says. I can tell Mom is still mad, but I also know she's not going to yell at me in front of everybody. So for now, at least, I'm safe.

As we file into the dining room area, I squeeze next to Bubbles. "What's going on?" she whispers in my ear.

"You got here just in time. I think my picture was about to end up on a milk carton!" I say, bumping into her.

We hightail it to the long dining room table, so we can eat dinner and practice the "soup-to-nuts situation." That's what we, the Cheetah Girls, call table manners.

My godfather—Galleria's dad, Mr. Garibaldi—is from Bologna, Italy, and he can cook like a chef. He says Europeans have better table manners than we do, so Bubbles knows everything. I have good table manners, too, because Abuela taught me. Dorinda, on the other hand, has table manners like a mischievous chimpanzee. That's why we are doing this dinner. She eats too fast and never looks up from her plate. One day, Aquanette, with her *boca grande*—her big mouth—blurted out to Dorinda, "Girl, the way you eat, you'd think you wuz digging for gold!"

Dorinda wasn't even embarrassed! She just giggled and said, "You gotta get it when you can." Do' Re Mi, as we call her, looks the youngest of all of us, and we all kind of treat her like our little sister. But in a lot of ways, she's lived through more than any of us.

Do' Re Mi's had kind of a hard life. She lives in a foster home uptown, with a lady named Mrs. Bosco and ten *other* foster kids. Dorinda says that sometimes they even steal food from each other's plates if Mrs. Bosco isn't looking.

So now that she is one of the Cheetah Girls, we're teaching Do' Re Mi how to "sip tea with a queen and eat pralines with a prince," as Bubbles says.

"*Mamacita*, the braids are *kicking*," Bubbles whispers to me, then touches my new headband and snaps it back into place.

"Ouch," I whimper, then giggle, adjusting my headband again.

"They got any leopard ones? How much was it?" Bubbles asks as we sit down at the table, on our best behavior.

"Eight duckets," I reply. "They came in green, and pink, and I think, black." Bubbles *loves* animal prints. She'd be happy if she could buy a headband that growled.

"You're gonna be broke and that ain't no joke," Do' Re Mi says, cutting her eyes at me. "How much money do you have left from what we earned at the Kats and Kittys show?"

"Not enough to buy an outfit for the *lonchando*," I say, cutting my eyes back. Compared to her, I've always had it easy—Mom and Dad always got me lots of things. Even now that they're not together, I can usually get what I want, up to a point. But see, I guess Princess

Pamela was right about me being "royalty," because nothing ever seems to be enough for me. I never met a store I didn't like, *está bien?* I never had a ducket that I didn't spend first chance I got. And now, my first "duckets in a bucket" for doing what I always dreamed of doing—singing with Bubbles onstage—are drizzling away *fast*.

"I didn't buy *anything*," Do' Re Mi grunts back at me. "I had to give all my money to Mrs. Bosco to help pay for her doctor bills."

"But we gotta look nice for the big meeting, don't we?" I moan. "We can't have you showin' up in old clothes from Goodwill!"

"Shoot, don't worry about it," Aqua huffs. "We ain't gotta impress nobody yet. Let's see what Mr. Jackal Johnson can do for *us* first."

"What do managers do, anyway?" Do' Re Mi asks.

"Nowadays, they just get you record deals and book you on tours," Bubbles explains to us. "You know, back in the day of groups like the Supremes and The Jackson Five, managers taught you everything, just like in charm school. How to talk, dress, sing, do interviews. That's what Mom says."

"Word. Well, maybe Mr. Jackal Johnson is just a jackal who'll make us cackle!" sighs Do' Re Mi, making a joke from one of the lines of Bubbles's song "Wanna-be Stars in the Jiggy Jungle."

After we stop giggling, I add, "Yes, but they are still talking about our show at the Klub."

"That's right. We are all that, and Mr. Jackal Johnson knows it." Aqua pulls out a nail file from her backpack to saw down her white frosted tips, which are covered with dollar-sign rhinestone decals. It's her trademark. She's "on the money"—get it?

"Aqua, you are not filing your nails at the table. That is so ticky-tacky!" screams Bubbles, then slaps her hand. "We're supposed to be learning table manners here—this is a big meeting and greeting, Miss 'press on.'"

"At least she ain't whipping out a Big Mac from her backpack," Do' Re Mi quips, making a joke about the twins because they always carry food or hot sauce with them.

"No Big Macs in my backpack, just got room for my dreams," Galleria says out loud, grooving to her own rhythm. Then she whips out her Kitty Kat notebook and starts writing furiously. "That's a song!"

"Shhh, my mom is m-a-a-d!" I whisper to her, then turn to Do' Re Mi. "To answer your question, I only have about thirty-seven duckets left!"

"That's all!?" the four of them say, ganging up on me.

"I knew you went and bought those Flipper shoes! You didn't fool me, Miss Fib-eroni!" says Bubbles, who is always supposed to be on my side but hasn't been lately.

"I don't care if you don't like them, I think they're *la dopa*!" I protest, talking about the sandals I bought the other day behind Bubbles's back. See, we were hanging out at the Manhattan Mall on 34th Street, and I saw them at the Click Your Heels shoe store. They are made out of vinyl, and have a see-through heel with plastic goldfish inside.

"I don't know why Auntie Juanita wants you to be a buyer, 'cuz you are a shopaholic waiting to happen," Bubbles quips. She calls my mom "Auntie" even though we aren't related. But we are just like sisters. Bubbles has a big mouth, but I'm used to that because she always used to back me up when my mouth wrote a check I couldn't cash. "Now what are you gonna do for a dress for our big *lonchando* with Mr. Johnson?"

"I don't know," I say, feeling like I want to burst out crying. "I've got these great diamond earrings Princess Pamela gave me, and those great shoes . . . but no dress. Bubbles, you still got some duckets left?"

Bubbles whips out her cheetah wallet to show us that she still has the money we earned from performing at the Kats and Kittys show stuffed inside. "I got all the duckets in this bucket, baby," she says, flossin'. "I'm not buying *nada*—and definitely no Prada!"

"Word, Galleria. Your wallet looks like it's having triplets," Do' Re Mi quips. She *would* be impressed.

"Maybe you could lend me some till our next gig?" I start to say, but Galleria cuts me off.

"No way, Miss Cuchifrito!" she says, putting the wallet back in her bag. "Duckets just fly through your fingers, *girlita*. I'd never see mine again. Maybe you ought to just borrow a dress from somebody—or make one, even!"

Just then, my mom comes into the dining room, so we all shut up about money. My mom puts the piping hot *panecitas* and butter on the table. These little rolls are my favorite. Do' Re Mi grabs one and starts spreading butter on the whole *panecita*, then does a chomp-aroni like Toto, and eats the whole thing!

"At least you're using a knife," I say, being *sarcástico*, then giggle. Everyone looks at me, because Do' and I are very close now. We talk on the phone a lot, and I even help her with her Spanish homework. So I guess I'm the one who's supposed to get this choo-choo train in motion.

"Do' Re Mi, watch this," I say, trying to be nice to her. "Break off a piece of the roll, then butter it and put the knife back across the plate like this."

"Word. I got it." Do' Re Mi giggles, then makes fun and starts spreading butter on the bread—oh so delicately, like a real phony baloney.

"You're on a roll, *churlita*!" I crack, then cover my mouth because I'm talking with food in it—and my mom has walked back in the dining room with the platter of *arroz con pollo*. She gives me a look that says, "I'm not finished with you yet." Aqua and Angie are giggling up a storm, like they think it's funny Do' Re Mi has to learn how to eat butter on a roll.

"Don't you two worry, we're gonna steam

roll over *your* choo-choo train, too," Bubbles warns them.

See, me, Bubbles, and Do' Re Mi have *tan coolio* style. We all go to Fashion Industries High School. The twins, who go to Performing Arts, dress, well, kinda corny, and act even cornier.

"Now, assuming Miss Cuchifrito here can make herself an outfit, all we have to do to get the Cheetah Girls on track is get you two some new do's—and outfits you can't wear at church!" Bubbles loves to tease the twins, who are unidentical but very much alike.

"Oh, and I got some virtual reality for you two," I add.

"Virtual reality?" Aqua says, taking her pink-flowered paper napkin off her lap and patting her juicy lips.

"I got the *Miss Wiggy Virtual Makeover* CD-ROM. It has one hundred fifty hairdos we can try, and one of them has just got to be fright, I mean, right for you!"

"We could do a sleepover here the night before our *lonchando*, right, Chuchie?" Bubbles asks. "That way we could take care of the do's right before the luncheon."

"I don't know about that," I say, croaking. "My mom's kinda down on me even *bein'* a Cheetah Girl. Maybe we better do it at your house." I roll my eyes at Bubbles, then toward the den next door, where my mom is talking on the phone to Mr. Tycoon in Paris.

I'm scared for my crew to leave, because then I will have to be alone with her. I take a deep breath, which is what Drinka Champagne, our vocal coach, tells us we have to do to help our singing voices stay strong.

After today's craziness with my *madre, lonchando* with Mr. Jackal Johnson will be a piece of cake. A piece of Princess Pamela's pound cake . . .

Later that night, I'm on the Internet chatting with my Cheetah Girls crew, when I hear my mom yelling over the phone to my dad. "I have a prediction for that *Princess Pamela*," my mom says all *sarcástico* into the phone receiver. "If *she* doesn't stay away from *my* daughter, The Wicked Witch of the Yeast is gonna slice her up like that cheesy pound cake she sells!" my mom snarls, then hangs up the phone. Mom always has to have the last word. I hear her bare feet pounding down the hallway.

"*Ciao* for now!" I type furiously on the keyboard. That's the signal we use when a grown-up is coming. I run to my bed and open up my history book. All I need is for my mom to see what I'm talking about with my crew on the Internet, and she may figure out a way to stop that, too.

I know she's about to come in, and I'm dreading the screaming fight we're about to have. But to my total surprise, the knock on my door is so low I almost don't hear it.

"What!" I yell, pretending that maybe I think it's Pucci.

"Can I come in?" Mom asks, in a voice so soft and sweet I barely recognize her.

"Sure, *Mamí*," I say more quietly.

When she walks into my room, she is smiling at me. Now I feel guilty for thinking bad thoughts about her. I've been assuming she was going to get on my case about every single thing in my life, and here she is, being sweet and nice.

"Hi, *Mamí*," I say, trying to act normal.

"Hi. What are you up to? You and the Cheetah Girls have been talking in the chat room, right?"

She is still smiling! Weird.

"Yeah." I giggle, shutting the cover of my history book. No use pretending now. Besides, it doesn't seem to be necessary. She's obviously not mad—but why? *Qué pasa?*

"I've been wondering—what are you going to wear for the lunch meeting with Mr. Johnson, Chuchie?" Mom asks me, plopping down on my pink bedspread. She then crosses her legs, like she is practicing a pose for the Chirpy Cheapies Catalog. My mom used to be a model, you know. Right now, she has put her wavy hair up in a ponytail. She almost looks like she could be my big sister instead of my mother.

"*Yo no sé*," I answer. "I don't know. I really don't have anything good to wear."

"Well, why don't you go ahead and order that green leopard pantsuit from Oophelia's catalog," she says with a satisfied smirk.

"Well, I can't buy it, because I only have thirty-seven dollars left from the money I got from the show," I say, kinda nervous. Don't get the wrong idea—I didn't just buy shoes and headbands, okay? I also bought a new laser printer for my computer, so that we, the Cheetah Girls, can make flyers for our shows—if we have any more.

"I know you don't have any money left, but I'm glad you bought a printer. So the outfit is on me. A little present. Here," Mom says, holding out her credit card. "You can use my credit card and order that one outfit."

I sit there frozen, not even able to breathe. This is like, unbelievable! My mom offering to let *me*, the shopaholic deluxe, use her credit card? What is up here?

"You sure?" I ask nervously, not daring to take it, for fear I'll be struck by lightning or something like that.

"Yes, I'm sure. I've been thinkin' about it all day. You and I haven't been spending enough time together lately—what with me bein' with my new boyfriend, and you hangin' with the Cheetah Girls. I miss bein' close."

I smile. "Me too, *Mami*."

"And I know how much this lunch meeting means to you and the girls. So I decided I want you to look your very best."

"Wow" is all I can say. I can feel the tears of gratitude welling in my eyes.

My mom looks up at the ceiling. "And it just bothers me that that *bruja* Pamela has been pushing her way into your heart, trying to buy your affection with diamond earrings and such. If anybody's going to buy you nice things, it's going to be me."

So *that's* it! "But, *Mami*—"

"Now, you just tell her you can't accept them, and that she's to stop giving you expensive gifts. It puts a wedge between you and me, baby, and we don't want that."

"But—"

"Now, now," she says, stroking my braids. "I can afford to get you even nicer earrings, if that's what you want."

"I can't return them, *Mami*," I say, holding my ground now that I know what she's after. So, all this niceness is just a trick, to try and turn me against Pamela! Well, it won't work. If people I like want to give me things, I should be allowed to accept them. "I can't and I won't!"

"All right," *Mami* says, seeing she can't win on this one. "You can keep the earrings. But from now on, no more gifts from that *bruja*, you hear?"

"Yes, *Mami*," I say, grabbing the compromise when I can get it. "Can I still buy the outfit?"

"Of course, baby," she says, smiling again,

although it looks more forced now than it did before. "I want you to look beautiful for your big meeting."

"But I thought you didn't even want me to *be* in the Cheetah Girls!" I point out. Then I want to kick myself for bringing it up. Why couldn't I just keep my *boca grande*—my big mouth— shut for once?

Incredibly, it doesn't seem to bother her. "I think it's just a phase you're going through, *mi hija*," she says, still smiling. "But since you insist on this singing nonsense, you may as well go all the way with it." She pushes the card into my hands and squeezes them. "Buy yourself the outfit. And remember who bought it for you—*me*, not Pamela—*está bien?*"

"*Sí, Mamí*," I say, giving her a big hug and kiss. I'm still mad at her for not believing in me, but at least she's showing me she loves me.

"Now, you know the rules, Chanel. You only order that one outfit. You give me the card back as soon as you're done. And don't you ask 'that woman' for anything ever again. *Entiendes?* You hear?"

Now she is wiping imaginary dust off my

altar table right next to the window. My altar table is covered with a pretty white tablecloth. On top of it, there are candles and offerings to the patron saints—fruits, nuts, and little prayer notes.

"I didn't ask Pamela for anything," I whine, making the cross-my-heart-and-hope-to-die sign across my chest. "She just gave the earrings to me!"

"Well, *don't* accept anything else. And if your father asks you anything, don't tell him what I told you. *Entiendes?*" Mom asks me—again. Now I'm really getting annoyed.

"*Está bien.* I won't. I promise," I respond. Anything to make her stop being such a policeman. "And thank you sooooo much! Letting me charge a new outfit is the best present anybody ever got me!"

I give her another hug, and that seems to do the trick. She flashes me a big smile, kisses me on the forehead, and heads for the door.

When Mom finally leaves my room, a sudden feeling of total bliss comes over me. The credit card feels sleek and powerful in my hand, and I'm anxious to get my shopping groove on. Prada or *nada*, baby! Okay, so I am

rolling more with the *nada* than the Prada—
but that is all gonna change with one phone
call!

As I flip through the catalog, looking at all
the dozens of things I'm longing to own, I hum
to myself, "Oooh, Oophelia's! I'm feeling ya!"

Chapter 3

I have never held Mom's credit card in my hot little hands before. Never. And now, the hologram on its face seems to wink at me, casting a witch's spell over me. I dial the 800 number and follow the computer instructions, punching in numbers here and there until I get to speak to a real-live person.

Meanwhile, I am thinking about poor Dorinda. She must feel so down about not being able to keep the duckets from our gig. It's so unfair that she had to give the money to her foster mom. My heart goes out to her. Surely, my mom wouldn't want us to lose out on making a deal with Mr. Johnson just because Do' Re Mi came dressed in rags!

I decide then and there to make one tiny little exception to Mom's rule. After all, she said I couldn't buy anything else—but that meant *for me*, didn't it? When the operator picks up, I order two of the green leopard outfits—one in my size, and one in Dorinda's. I give the credit card number to the lady on the phone, and as I do, my gaze wanders to the pages of the catalog. So many other great things, things I've always wanted, and will never have another chance to get . . .

What would it hurt to borrow just a little of Mom's credit to stock up on stuff? When we sign with Mr. Johnson, it will be no time till we're making big duckets from gigs, maybe even a record deal! I can pay my mom back before she even knows I've spent the money!

"Will that be all, ma'am?" the voice asks me.

"Uh . . . no," I hear myself say. "No . . . just one or two more things . . ."

Do' Re Mi looks so "money" in the new outfit I bought her. And on top of that, Bubbles's mom, who is my *madrina*—my godmother—since birth (and the best godmother in the whole world) made *her* a green leopard pantsuit to match ours for our meeting with Mr. Johnson!

Aqua is wearing a black and white checked blazer with a red shirt and black skirt. Angie has on a denim suit with a hot pink turtleneck.

"At least they don't look like they're going to church," Bubbles giggles to me, sneaking a look in the mirror that covers one whole wall of The Hydrant Restaurant on Fifteenth Street, where we are meeting Mr. Johnson.

When we first tried to tell Angie and Aqua what to wear for the meeting, Aqua got all huffy and said, "*We* are saving *our* money to go home to Houston for Thanksgiving!" The twins are headed south for the holidays—in more ways than one!

"I feel so large and in charge, I'm loving it—and you all, too!" Bubbles says. "That was so nice of Auntie Juanita to let you buy Do' Re Mi a pantsuit, too, Chuchie!"

Okay, so I told Bubbles a little fib-eroni. I didn't want her to think that I did . . . well, what I actually did. I'll have to straighten her out soon, though, before she opens her *boca grande*—her big mouth—and spills the refried beans to my mom.

The table is covered with a bright-red linen tablecloth, and six red linen napkins placed perfectly apart. Right in the middle of the round table is a big glass vase with lots of pink roses, my favorite *flores*.

"You nervous?" I ask Do' Re Mi, then I add giggling, "I feel like I'm at a seance and the table is gonna lift up any second!"

Mr. Johnson has gone to check our jackets. Yes, we have it like that. There is a waiter dressed in white, standing near our table. He smiles at me when I look in his direction.

"Somebody pinch me, pleez, so I can wake up!" I giggle, then look around at all the people who are having lunch at The Hydrant. I take the book of matches with the name of the restaurant out of the ashtray, and stick it in my cheetah backpack for a souvenir. All around us are grown-ups, and they are all dressed *adobo down*. The lady at the table next to us is sitting by herself.

"She must be waiting for *El Presidente*," I whisper to Bubbles. The lady is wearing a big hat with a black peacock feather poking her almost in the eye! She looks at us and smiles. Then the peacock lady puts on lipstick without even looking in a mirror! "She definitely has the skills to pay the bills," Bubbles quips.

Do' Re Mi looks like she is getting nervous, too, because she is reading the menu like she is studying for a test at school. Then all of a sudden she whispers to me, "What should I order?"

"Just don't get spaghetti marinara," I whisper back.

"Do' Re Mi, try the *penne arrabbiata*—that's the pasta cut on the slanty tip with red *pepper-on-cino*."

"What's *that*?" Do' Re Mi quizzes Bubbles.

"Those crushed red pepper flakes that Angie loves to put on pizza. You can hang with that!" Bubbles blurts out.

"Here he comes," whispers Angie.

"Ladies, order to your heart's delight," Mr. Johnson commands us, as he sits down and puts the napkin in his lap. We all do the same thing. Do' Re Mi flaps the napkin really loud when she opens it, like it has wings, but we act like we don't notice. Mr. Johnson is wearing a yellow tie brighter than a Chiquita banana, and his two front teeth don't talk to each other. He has a *really* big gap.

"This place is majordomo dope," Bubbles exclaims, looking around once more.

"Yeah, and I've done some pretty major-domo deals here, as you would say," chuckles Mr. Johnson, looking at Bubbles. "So you're the writer of the group, huh?" he asks her.

"Yup," Bubbles says, smiling. Bubbles isn't afraid of anything. She just acts like herself. He obviously just looks to her as if she is the leader. Which *is* kinda true anyway. We wouldn't be a group, I think, if it wasn't for Bubbles. But I don't want Bubbles to be the *only* leader, because it was my idea too to *be* in a group, so that counts for something.

Today Bubbles is wearing her hair really straight and parted down the middle. I put her extensions in myself, so I know they won't come out even if Hurricane Gloria flies in from Miami!

"Pucci would love this place," I giggle, looking at the red brick walls. My mom says The Hydrant is a one-star bistro. I don't know what that means, but now that she has Mr. Tycoon for a boyfriend, she goes to places, she says, where they don't even have prices on the menu. I guess this one doesn't count, because it does.

"You know, this place used to be a fire-house," says Mr. Johnson. "Lotta action coming down that pole." Mr. Johnson is looking over in the direction of the big metal pole that goes all the way up the ceiling. "Back in the day, there were some pretty bad torch jobs in the city. Buildings burning down all the time. It kept firemen pretty busy, but things have gotten better, and they closed the firehouse down two years ago."

The waiters are sliding down the pole now, bringing food from the kitchen above. "Tourists love that," Mr. Johnson chuckles.

"I wonder if the waiters get scared," Aquanette asks, touching her pin curl, which is laid down and fried to the side of her face.

"Well, let's clear away the okeydokey and talk some bizness, here," Mr. Johnson chuckles. He definitely has more rhymes than Dr. Seuss. He looks at all five of us and says, "As your manager, I want you to know that I'm going to forego all production costs for a demo, and get you in the studio with some real heavy-hitting producers, arrangers, and engineers."

"Can we do some of my songs?" Bubbles asks, always looking out for *número una*.

"Not right away, Galleria. Now, I know your songs are smokin', 'cuz I heard you girls singing them the night I saw you perform at Cheetah-Rama, but let's start with the producers' songs." Mr. Johnson takes a sip of bubbly water from his glass, then licks his lips. "Pumpmaster Pooch has worked with some really big artists, so he knows how to turn a song into an instant hit," he says.

I hope the water doesn't make me burp, I think, as I sip some from my glass, too.

"Who has Pumpmaster Pooch worked with?" Do' Re Mi asks.

"Well, I don't want to say right now, because none of the songs have gotten picked up just yet. You girls have to understand. There is a one in a million chance for a record to turn gold, but if you go into the studio with producers who've got the Midas touch, you're likely to turn that song into gold."

"What happens to the songs after we finish them?" Angie asks.

"We—that means I—have to get your demo to the record companies. It takes a lot of wheeling-and-dealing, but don't worry about it, 'cuz it ain't no thing like a chicken wing."

We look at each other like we've just eaten some Green Eggs and Ham, or something.

Mr. Johnson catches on to our confusion. "What I mean is, I have a serious setup at Hyena Records. Me and the A&R guy—that's the artist development person, who goes out scouting the country for talent just like you— go way back. *And* I've been doing business with Mr. Hyena, the company president, for years. After he gets a taste of that growl power y'all got going on, he'll be chomping at the bit to sign some superlistic talent such as yourselves. Just let me handle it."

I sit there wondering how Mr. Johnson can talk so fast without even taking a breath. I wish Drinka could see him in action.

"Hyena Records. Who do they have on the label?" Do' Re Mi asks, all curious. When Mr. Johnson turns his head toward her, I motion quickly to Angie with my hand. She has a piece of green something stuck on a tooth in the front, and she is just smiling her head off.

"Now, they're not what they used to be back in the day," Mr. Johnson says, his pinky finger dangling to the wind as he sips his water. "But nothing is like it used to be in the music biz."

"Ooh, this is bubbly," Aqua says, her eyes popping open as she puts her glass down.

"Bubbles. That's me," Galleria says, starting to sway. "The Cheetah Girls are cutting a demo, so take a memo, all you wanna-be stars trying to get a whiff of what it feels like," Bubbles giggles. She is flossin' for Mr. Johnson.

"That's very good, Galleria." He chuckles. "You do that off the top of your head?"

All of this is going to Bubbles's head, I think. I wish I knew how to make up songs like her. Then Mr. Johnson would like me, too.

The waiter comes and takes our orders. After he leaves, Mr. Johnson whips a manila envelope out of his pocket and opens it. Inside are five pieces of paper.

"Listen, before our food gets here, I want each of you to give one of these to your parents. Have them look it over, then sign it. You can give it back to me the next time we meet, in the studio."

"What is it?" Do' Re Mi asks.

"It's no big deal—just a temporary agreement—a standard management contract, so we can get started right away on your demo. It's your time and my dime—so let's not waste it, Cheetah Girls!" Mr. Johnson quips.

He sure is making moves like a jackal. Just like his name. I guess I'll have my dad look it over. He is good with business. I wish I could give it to Princess Pamela, too. She is smart like that. But Mom would really go off on me if she found out I did that.

"Enough business for now," Mr. Johnson says with a big, gap-toothed smile. "Why don't you girls tell me all about yourselves?"

And we do . . . oh, do we ever!

Chapter 4

Things went really well today at our first business *lonchando*, I think to myself as I'm lying on my bed, clacking the heels of my black patent leather loafers together. I have the keyboard on the bed, and I'm yapping on the Internet with Bubbles, Angie, and Aqua. Dorinda is coming over so we can do our homework together. Meanwhile, I'm trying to get them to help me with this Princess Pamela situation, and end the frustration.

"I just don't think it's fair that you can't see Pamela, and I'm not being square," Bubbles says.

Angie has an idea: "Dag on, we got so many problems. We better have Cheetah Girls council meetings, so we can give each other advice, instead of rehearsing all the time and talking about being wanna-be stars!"

"It's a done wheel-a-deal," Bubbles types back, imitating Mr. Johnson. "Let's have Cheetah Girls council meetings once a week!"

My bedroom door is open, so I don't hear when my mom walks right in. "Chuchie," she says, almost scaring me.

"Oh, hi, *Mami*," I say, hoping she isn't trying to peep my chat.

"You forgot to give me back my credit card," she says.

"Oh! Right!" I fall all over myself going to my dresser drawer, and take it out. Handing it to her, I say, "*Mami*, that was so generous of you letting me get that outfit."

She smiles and gives me a kiss. "The meeting was good, huh?" she asks. Then she sits down on my bed.

"*Sí, Mami*. Thanks so much."

She hands me back the management agreement form that Mr. Johnson wanted us to sign. "As long as you do your schoolwork and finish high school, *then* go to college, you can stay with this little group of yours. Just don't get any ideas that this is for real, okay?" she says, taking my comb and starting to comb her hair.

"Okay, *Mami*," I growl back.

My mom just won't get it into her head that I am very serious about being a Cheetah Girl, or that it means everything to me. I know I will do whatever my mom wants me to do, but on the other hand, I have to do what's right for me.

"You better let your father see that agreement, too, or he'll have a fit," Mom adds, while she looks in my mirror and combs out her hair.

That's how she gets when she talks about my dad. It makes me so sad that they fight all the time. I'll tell you one thing, though. She is not going to keep me away from Princess Pamela.

"Yes, *Mami*," I reply.

Deep in my heart, I know what I want. I want to be a Cheetah Girl and travel all over the world. Then I'm going to buy Abuela Florita a house away from Washington Heights and near the ocean so she can dream about the D.R.—the Dominican Republic, where she was born. I'm gonna live near her, so we can see each other more often.

Mom interrupts my *gran fantasía*. "So. You're going to the studio tomorrow, huh?" she asks.

"Yeah, I'm kinda nervous about making a demo tape," I explain.

"What's that?" she asks me, then looks at herself sideways in the mirror.

"It's a tape of songs that shows how we sing, so a record company will give us a deal. Maybe it's not a whole tape, but it's something."

"Mmm," Mom says, getting up off the bed. "You and your crazy dreams."

She leaves my room and goes back to the exercise studio. Lately, she has become an exotic dancing fanatic. She says it's great exercise, better than jogging. Her tummy is as flat as my chest, so it must be true. She's looking good, and she's got a boyfriend with *mucho dinero*, so why is she so worked up about Princess Pamela?

I ponder the situation. What am I gonna do? I love Princess Pamela, and she is so nice to me, but I know it makes my mom unhappy that I am close to her.

Our Cheetah Girls crew council is a good idea, for starters. Maybe I could ask Bubbles's mom, Dorothea, my *madrina*, who is super *simpática*, what I should do. But, then again, she andMom are friends since their modeling days, so maybe I can't trust her with everything.

Then it hits me! I get *un buen* idea. I can call Princess Pamela's Psychic Hotline, disguise my voice, and ask *her* what to do!

I dial the 900-PRINCESS number and hold my breath. I can feel my heart pounding through my chest like a secret agent on a mission. "I like truffles, not R-r-u-ffles," I hum to myself, rolling my Rs. Everybody at Drinka's voice and dance studio is so jealous because they can't roll their Rs like I do.

That is my *cultura* for you, I smile to myself, as I take a piece of Godiva chocolate from the box Bubbles's mom gave each of us for Halloween. I've hidden the box from Pucci's little grubby hands.

A voice machine comes on, telling me the Princess is out, and to call back later. Great. There's never a psychic around when you really need one.

I get off the bed, and put a few oranges on my little altar table as an offering for Santa Prosperita. I don't know if she is a real saint, but she is *my* saint, and if you want something bad enough, you can get it, Princess Pamela says. She should know.

"I know it's not right to ask for anything

material, but *por favor*, I need just one little thing," I whisper to my Santa Prosperita. "Just one little Prada bag!"

See, the Kats and Kittys Klub is selling raffle tickets for community service. Each of the members has to sell as many raffle tickets as possible, and all the proceeds are going to the needy. The best part: the grand prize is two Prada bags! I have got to have them—at least one of them! The only problem is, I'm not too lucky at these kind of things. So I figure I'd better buy a *lot* of tickets.

Of course, that could be a problem, since my pile of duckets is now down to just fourteen. But hey—no *problemo*! I go to my math notebook and open it up to the last page. There, I have written the number and expiration date of my mom's credit card!

I know what you're thinking, but it's not true—I only wrote it down just in case I lost the card, or forgot the number or something! And I *meant* to cross it out when I gave the card back, but I haven't had the chance. And now . . .

Well, look. It's a worthy cause, *está bien?* All those poor needy people in the world—how could I not reach out to help them?

I'm sure my mom won't mind, especially since, if I win, I'll definitely give her one of the Prada bags. Besides, I'll pay her back for everything, once the Cheetah Girls hit it big—which we're sure to do, now that we're signing on with Mr. Johnson and making a demo tape! I mean, how long could it be before we're rolling in *dinero*?

I call up the Kats and Kittys Klub. Mrs. Goodge, the secretary, gets on the line. "Oh, hello, there, Chanel! What can I do for you?"

I tell her.

"A hundred tickets? Why, Chanel, that's very generous of your mother!"

"Yes it is, Mrs. Goodge," I say. "My mom is one of the most generous people there is, and she really cares about needy people, too!"

"How will she be paying? Cash or check?" Mrs. Goodge asks.

"Um, she gave me her credit card number to give you," I say.

"Oh. I see . . . well, I suppose that'll be all right," she says.

I give her the number.

"That's one hundred raffle tickets at two dollars each, for a total of two hundred dollars.

Thank you so much, Chanel—and be sure to thank your mother for us!"

"I'll do that, Mrs. Goodge," I say.

Yeah, right. Sure I will. That would not be a smart thing to do, now, would it? I hang up, feeling guilty but excited. I'm sure to win the Prada bags, with odds like these. A hundred tickets! How can I miss?

I flop back on the bed and flip through my Oophelia's catalog once again, even though I know every page by heart. How can I pass up these lime green suede boots? I wonder. . . .

My mom is gonna kill me. Well, at the rate the group is growing, the Cheetah Girls will probably be rich soon, so I can pay my mom back then, I tell myself. I pick up the phone and punch in a number, and I hear my own voice ordering the lime green suede boots from the Oophelia's catalog operator.

Then I spot something else I just have to have. Ooh, this rug is so cute. It has a big *mono*, monkey face on it. I love monkeys! Ooh, it has a matching blue stool with a *mono* on it, too! I guess it won't hurt if I order just one more thing. Mom won't mind, I tell myself. She knows my old daisy area rug has seen better days. It looks like someone has tiptoed through the tulips on it.

Mom *did* say not to use her credit card, but I don't think she will mind, since it's something for my room. At least that's what I tell myself. And if she does mind, too bad. I deserve a new rug, and the stool matches, so I just have to get that, too.

I am so good at making my voice sound grown-up, the operator never asks me anything. The stool is $156, and the rug is $38. Mono better do some tricks with a banana for this kinda money, I think, giggling to myself as I place the order. "Does it come in any other color?" I ask.

"No, just blue with the red monkey design," the operator replies.

The stool is real leather, not pleather, so I decide to go for it. But I have to have the cheetah picture frame, too, I suddenly realize. I *need* a new frame for my Confirmation picture sitting on the dresser. It is my favorite picture, not counting the one of me at my sixth-birthday party, standing with the piñata that I busted open all by myself. In it, I am making a face because I got a terrible stomachache after I ate everything that fell out of the piñata.

In the Confirmation picture, I'm wearing the holy red robe for the ceremony. This is the color that symbolizes the fire of the Holy Spirit. Abuela has her arm around me and she is smiling. My silver cross is draped across the picture frame, which is supposed to be silver, but it has changed colors and looks old. My mom picked it out. I wonder if she knew it was fake silver. Surely she'd want me to have a better one if she knew. A picture like this one deserves the best frame there is!

So I order it, along with everything else. I'm feeling dizzy from my little shopping spree—dizzy and happy, and a little bit scared. What if my mom finds out before I get enough money to pay her back?

Well, she won't, that's all, I tell myself. I'll just make sure she doesn't. I quickly shut my math notebook and put it away.

"Will that be all, ma'am?" the operator asks. Just as I'm about to say yes, I realize that I really need a new outfit to go to the recording studio, so I make the operator wait until I pick one out of the catalog. She adds it to the total, and when she reads me back a list of what I've bought, I almost chicken out, it's so much money.

But then, I think to myself, Why should I care if Mom gets mad? She's always mad at me anyway. No matter what I do, it's wrong—"Don't talk with that witch Pamela! Don't take the Cheetah Girls too seriously! Don't do this, don't do that . . ." Well, too bad for her. I'll do what I want.

"Yes, that will be fine," I tell the operator.

That's what you get, *Mamí*, for trying to control every move I make!

I have just hung up, when Pucci comes into my room without even knocking. "Get out, Pucci!" I yell at him. I hate when he does that. We aren't little anymore, you know? "What do I have to do to get rid of you?" I blurt out.

"Get me a dog. I want a dog!" Pucci giggles. "How come we can't have a dog?"

"You know *Mamí* isn't gonna let us have a dog, Pucci. Why are you bothering me?"

And then it hits me. Why *can't* Pucci have a dog? *I* want one, too. Nothing against Snuggly-Wiggly Pooch, but a real dog would be *la dopa*! Mom's always complaining how allergic she is, but there must be some kind of dog that doesn't shed. Why can't we get one of those? Yeah . . .

now, there's a great idea! Right away, I start to cook up how to get us a real-live dog.

Meanwhile, I don't feel like doing my ballet exercises, but I know I've got to, to help keep my body strong. Changing into my pink leotard, I groan to myself. All this shopping is exhausting, but hey—a Cheetah Girl's day is never done!

Chapter 5

These days, the Cheetah Girls are really living *la vida loca*—the crazy life. Rehearsals, school, homework, and, for me, fighting with my mom, and spending secret nights on the Psychic Hot Line with Princess Pamela, or shopping on the phone and ordering from Oophelia's catalog.

Thank goodness, history class is the last of the day. At four o'clock, we have to meet Mr. Johnson at Snare-a-Hare Recording Studios in Times Square. He has arranged for us to have a recording session with this Big Willy producer, Pumpmaster Pooch.

We did find out about Pumpmaster's "credits." He did the rap remix for the Sista Fudge single, "I'll Slice You Like a Pound Cake." That's something, huh? That song is one of Princess Pamela's favorites. It makes her giggle and makes me wiggle.

Speaking of Princess Pamela, I've been running up the phone bill calling her 900 number. I've been getting some pretty strange advice, too—she's been telling me to watch out for animals. I wonder what she means by that. . . .

Maybe I should forget about the dog I've been planning to get Pucci. Or maybe it's the Cheetahs I ought to stay away from. No, that can't be. Maybe Princess Pamela is off the mark this time. After all, she doesn't know who she's talking to. I've been disguising my voice, so maybe that's throwing off her predictions. Still, it's been bothering me, and I just can't figure it out.

I almost asked Princess Pamela about it yesterday, when I gave her the management agreement to pass on to my dad. But that would have been giving myself away, and I didn't want it getting back to my dad that I'd been running up the phone bill to get advice I could have gotten for free!

I also wanted to tell Princess Pamela about

all the money I've been spending, and get her advice on that, too—but I knew it would make Mom mad if she found out I'd been asking Princess Pamela for advice, let alone that I'd been using her credit card and running up her phone bill!

"How much did Mr. Johnson say it costs for an hour at the recording studio?" Do' Re Mi asks, bringing me back to reality. We are at our lockers after school, getting ready to go over to the studio for our recording session.

"The studio? It costs a lot, but we don't have to pay for it," I answer.

Me, Bubbles, and Do' Re Mi are looking *muy caliente* today—hot, hot, hot! We're all wearing matching red velvet jeans and crushed velvet leopard T-shirts from Oophelia's. Bubbles's mom paid for hers. I bought mine and Do' Re Mi's on my mom's credit card (surprise, surprise).

"Chuchie, you are lost in your own soap opera channel. What's the matter, *mamacita*, Snuggly-Wiggly Pooch ate your homework?" Bubbles chides me, putting her arm around my shoulders. "What's wrong? You're not giggling, and that's kinda like Toto not begging for food. Ya know what I mean, prom queen?"

I poke Bubbles in the side, because Derek Hambone and Mackerel Johnson are standing by their lockers across the hall. "Duckets in the bucket alert!" I whisper in Bubbles's ear.

Like the Road Runner, Bubbles makes a bee-line to hit up the dynamic duo, and make them buy Kats and Kittys raffle tickets.

"Hit 'em up, Galleria!" Do' Re Mi says, egging Bubbles on.

Derek is this new "brotha from Detroit," as he calls himself, and the word is, he comes from a family that owns the biggest widget fac-tory in the East—*mucho dinero, mamacita*!

"Derek, my Batman with a plan. Buy a raffle ticket for me and part with two dollars for a good cause. You, too, Mackerel. Come on, I'll let you two touch my vest—it's national velvet. Feel the pile!" Bubbles urges them.

"Awright," Derek says, reaching for the ticket, but then he looks at it, reads about the Prada prize, and says, "Cheetah Girl, you expect me to get jiggy in the jungle with a *Prada* bag? I'm not going out like that."

"Oh, come on, *schemo*, you ain't gonna win the raffle, anyway, just part with the two duckets!" Bubbles says, pouting. Derek is such a *pobrecito*—a real dummy. He doesn't even know Bubbles is calling him a dodo bird in Italian. I *know* Derek isn't going to win, because I *better* win. No one else deserves that Prada bag more than I do! *"Prada or nada"* is the motto I live and die by.

"Awright, I'm gonna let you hit me up this time, Cheetah Girl, Derek says, like he is a loan officer at Banco Popular, "but you owe me *big-time* for this one." Reaching into his baggy jeans, I wonder if Derek is ever gonna find the bottom of his deep, baggy pockets. I wonder how the "Red Snapper" is gonna get his money off the hook.

See, Derek likes Bubbles—and he's always snapping at her bait—that's why we nick-named him "Red Snapper"—and also because his best friend is Mackerel Johnson. Derek is the only one of his posse who is large enough to become a member of the Kats and Kittys Klub, though. It costs $650 a year.

Mackerel smiles at me while he's bouncing to some tune in his peanut-sized head. He is so hyper, he looks like a Chihuahua bobbing his head up and down.

Oh, snapples, that's what I could get Pucci! "My mom can't say *nada* about a Chihuahua— they are so little, who could be allergic to them?

Meanwhile, Bubbles is still closing the deal. "Thank you, *schemo*," she smirks to Derek and Mackerel, stuffing their duckets into her chubby Cheetah wallet.

"Shame on you, too, Cheetah Girl. Just be ready when it's time to collect, awright?" Derek says, winking. Then he walks away with Mackerel.

"You got one of them dog books from the library, right?" I say to Do' Re Mi. I'm on a bowwow mission now.

"Yeah, why?" Do' Re Mi replies.

"Look up the breed Chihuahua and see if they shed hair."

"Word. Wait, they ain't got any hair," Do' Re Mi counters. She is so smart. The most booksmart of all of us.

"Look it up anyway," I giggle. "I think Miss Cuchifrito just got lucky. See, if Chihuahuas don't shed, then I can buy Pucci one for his birthday!"

"If you buy Pucci a dog, *you're* gonna end up at the dog pound for sure," Bubbles quips to me.

"And where you gonna get that kinda money?"

"It's three o'clock, y'all!" Do' Re Mi says, setting off down the hallway in her size zero velvet jeans. "We better get over to the studio, and start gettin' down!"

"Oh, snapples, I forgot to get the agreement back from Princess Pamela," I sigh to Bubbles.

"What's she doing with it?" Bubbles asks me, like she's saying, "Don't play with fire."

"I gave it to her so she could give it to my dad," I said. "I didn't have time to go all the way uptown, baby, okay? My mom is watching me like a hawk when she isn't doing her exotic dancing!"

"Mr. Johnson won't mind if you don't have the agreement. Just tell him we'll bring it to him the next time," Bubbles says, grabbing my arm and pulling me along. "Come on, *señorita*. We've got some singin' to do!"

Recording studios have more gadgets on the control board than I've ever seen in my life. "They got so many buttons, how do they know which ones to push?" I exclaim to Do' Re Mi, who is *muy fascinado* with anything *electrónico* or *en la Web*.

"That's why he's making the duckets," Bubbles smirks to the engineer, who is sitting at the board with headphones on.

Bubbles's mom, Dorothea, has come with us to the studio, but the twins haven't arrived yet.

"This is Kew, the engineer," Mr. Johnson says, introducing us as the Cheetah Girls. No matter how many times I hear our group's name, it sounds like *la música* to my ears. I love it!

"Mr. Johnson, can I speak to you for a minute?" Dorothea says. The two grown-ups go into another room—so they can talk business, I'm sure. Dorothea is all about the "Benjamins" and she doesn't play. She looks *la dopa* today, too. She is wearing a big leopard hat, and leopard boots that make her look taller than "The Return of the Fifty-Foot Woman"—even though she is only six feet tall. I wish *I* was that tall.

At last, the huggy bear twins have arrived!

"You know the Cheetah Girls rule: don't be late or we'll gaspitate!" Bubbles says, warning the twins as they hurriedly throw their cheetah backpacks on an empty chair in the studio.

"Dag on, y'all, just when we think we know how to get somewhere, they change the subway line on us!" Aqua laments, fixing her pin curl in place. Aquanette and Anginette still haven't learned their way around the Big Apple yet.

"You're 'Westies' now like me, so you'd better get with the IRT program," Do' Re Mi grunts. She lives on 116th, on the Upper West Side, and last summer, the twins moved from sunny Houston to 96th Street and Riverside Drive.

Like mine, their parents are "dee-vorced" (as Angie says in her Southern drawl), and the twins live with their dad. He must be kinda cool, 'cuz he pays for them to go to the beauty parlor twice a month to get their hair *and* nails done. I think they should pay me instead because I would give them *la dopa* hairstyles instead of the "shellac attack" curls they like so much. Sometimes less is more!

Today, the twins are wearing makeup, so they look kinda cute. Aqua and Angie are *café sin leche* color, and they love that white frost lipstick on their big, juicy lips. They are screaming for a Miss Wiggy! virtual makeover.

Mr. Johnson and Dorothea come back into the room. His beeper goes off, and he looks at it nervously. "I got a situation I gotta take care of," he says. "That is Mr. Hyena—I told you about him—he is the Big Willy at Hyena Records. Mrs. Garibaldi, Kew will look after you. And Pooch will get with you girls when he gets through," Mr. Johnson adds chuckling, never too nervous to get a rhyme out.

Pumpmaster Pooch is in the other room on his cell phone. We can see him through the big glass partition. He waves at us with his five-carat fingers. I mean, he is wearing enough gold rings to start a gold mine. Kew is busy fiddling with the keyboard, so the five of us sit and watch the music videos on MTV, which are playing on one of the monitors over our heads.

"*Ay, Dios mío*, Krusher's latest music video!" I whisper.

Dorothea goes into the room with Pumpmaster Pooch, so we relax a little. I feel so nervous!

"Krusher's got it going on," Do' Re Mi says, looking up at the monitor and grooving to Krusher's new single, "My Way or the Highway."

"Look at Chanel getting all goo-goo-eyed!" Do' Re Mi says.

"I'm saving my first kiss for him," I giggle to my crew.

"You better hope it ain't the first 'dis!'" Do' Re Mi sighs.

"Oh, *cállate la boca, Mamacita*. Be quiet." I sigh, then hum aloud, "*Yo tengo un coco* on Crusher."

"What's that mean?" Do' Re Mi asks, smirking and squinting her eyes.

"Look it up!" I heckle. "I'm just playing with you, Dor-r-r-inda, *Mami*," I say rolling my r's like I'm on a choo-choo train. "You won't find it in *el diccionario*. It means I have a crush on Krusher."

"Coco is cuckoo for Krusher," Bubbles heckles, making a play on my middle name.

"Watch out, Chuchie, this may be your last dance, last chance," Bubbles says, pointing her finger excitedly at the monitor.

The Krusher music video has ended, and now there is a commercial for a Krusher contest. "Are you the lucky girl who will win an all-expenses-paid date with R&B's hottest singer, and spend two fun-filled days and nights with Krusher in sunny Miami? What are you waiting for? Call 900-KRUSHER right now!"

"*Ay, Dios mío*! I'm gonna enter," I squeal, jumping up and down.

"Okay, Cuckoo Coco, get over it, because here comes the man," whispers Do' Re Mi, secretly pointing to Pooch, who is on the move toward us.

"Ladies, ladies, I'm sorry to keep you waiting," Pumpmaster Pooch says, rushing into the engineer's booth. He has on dark sunglasses and a hat, and a black windbreaker. I can tell he thinks he's kinda *chulo*, kind of cute, too.

"Now, I got a song you are gonna love. I've picked out some material for you—the type of songs that will get you a record deal, so just trust me on this," he says, talking with his five-carat hands the whole time. "Okay, let's do this."

Pooch tells Kew what tracks to put on, then takes us to the recording booth. The five of us stand in front of the microphones and put headphones on our heads. "We're gonna practice it a bit, then take it from the top when we're ready," Pooch says.

"Where are the musicians?" Angie asks, like she's been in a recording studio before.

"We're just gonna lay down some lead vocals

over the tracks first so you can get the hang of the song, ya dig?" Pumpmaster says, looking at Bubbles mostly, and the twins. The twins have been singing in church choirs since they're nine, so they always seem like they know what they're doing. "Then we lay down the background vocals and arrangements later. That's my job. We ready, Cheetah Girls?" Pumpmaster Pooch says, flashing a grin.

"We're ready!" we say together. I am so excited—I cannot believe that we, the Cheetah Girls, are already in the studio, recording. Okay, it's just a song for a demo, but you know what I mean, jelly bean.

"'I Got a Thing for Thugs'?" Bubbles says, scrunching up her nose as we read the lyrics off the sheet music that Pooch has handed out to us. "That sounds radickio!"

"Bubbles, let's just listen to them, okay?" I say, trying to calm her down because I know we are lucky to be here in the studio and not paying for it.

But after we finish rehearsing the same song fifty thousand times, we are so tired I never want to hear that song again. Bubbles is right. The song is *la wacka*! Bubbles looks like she is about to explode. I guess she thought we would be doing one of *her* songs.

Mr. Johnson, who has returned, comes in and congratulates us. "Ladies, you did a wonderful job. Now the car service is gonna come and take all of you right to your door."

"That song was wack-a-doodle," Bubbles says, pouting, when we are finally in the car with Dorothea. "It just wasn't *us*."

"Maybe once we do some of their songs, they'll let us record some of yours," I explain to Bubbles. She is *caliente* mad.

"What did you think, Mom?" Bubbles says, putting her head on Dorothea's shoulder.

"There is something about that Mr. Johnson that I don't like," Dorothea says, then leans back into the car seat. "I told him that I have to have the agreement looked over by a lawyer first, and that made him kind of nervous. If anything isn't right with that agreement, I'm gonna be so shady to Mr. Jackal Johnson the sun is gonna go down on him!"

Yawning, I put my head on Dorothea's other shoulder, and sigh. "Bubbles, you're right— that song *was* wack-a-doodle!" We giggle, then get real quiet for the rest of the way home.

I can't wait to get home and call 900-KRUSH-ER. I'm gonna call a hundred times if I have to, because I'm going win that date with Krusher and make my dreams come true.

That's what me and Bubbles always said when we were little. We would follow the yellow brick road no matter where it led us. Well, Miami, here I come!

Chapter 6

It's time for me to head uptown to Drinka Champagne's Conservatory. All five of us are now taking vocal lessons and dance classes there. Aqua and Angie don't need it, because they go to Laguardia Performing Arts High School and they get *la dopa* training all week, but it helps us to sing better together as a group. We also practice songs that Bubbles wrote—"Wanna-be Stars in the Jiggy Jungle" and "Welcome to the Glitterdome"—just in case Mr. Johnson and Pumpmaster Pooch decide to let us record them for our demo. Hey, you never know!

If I don't leave now, I'm gonna be late. Class starts at eleven o'clock, and Drinka does not play. If you walk in one minute late, she will stop everything and read you like *La Prensa*, our local Spanish newspaper, right in front of *everybody*. Now I'm mad at myself because I wanted to get to class early today, so I could show Drinka and the Cheetah Girls how much work I'm doing on my breathing exercises.

I spritz on my favorite perfume—Fetch, by Yves Saint Bernard (Princess Pamela bought it for my thirteenth birthday last year). I also spritz some Breath-So-Fresh spray in my throat. It makes me feel better, even though Bubbles says buying that stuff its like throwing "duckets down the drain."

I'm the one with the sensitive vocal chords, so I have to try whatever I can. Bubbles has a throat like the Tin Man. She can eat a plate of *arroz con pollo* with a bottle of hot sauce, sing for three hours straight, then still be able to blab her mouth on the phone till the break of dawn!

I look at the clock again. Hmmm. Maybe I can get one more call in to 900-KRUSHER before I go. I pick up my red princess phone, and start sweating as soon as I hear Krusher cooing in the background of the taped recording. I *have* to win this contest. My *corazón* would be broken if some other girl gets a date in Miami with my *papí chulo*, my sugar daddy. No—I can't think like this, or I will faint for real.

I listen to the recorded message for the tenth time in a row. The instructions are simple: you have to tell, in your own words, why you think you should win the date with Krusher.

I have a *buen* idea! I'll *sing* to Krusher on the phone. One of the Cheetah Girls songs! I betcha none of the other *mamacitas* calling could do that. It'll be my ace to first base.

"Hi, it's Chanel Simmons *again*," I say, giggling into the phone. Then I get kinda nervous. "I think I should win the Krusher contest because I know all the words to every song you've ever done. Right now, I'm gonna sing you one of the songs from my own group, the Cheetah Girls. . . . "

My *gran fantasía* is fumbled, though, because all of a sudden, I hear my mother hang up the phone in the hallway and scream my name really loud. "CHANEL! Get out here! *Apúrate!*" I almost faint for real, and I get a knot in my stomach like when I know I'm in *trouble*.

"*Ay dios, por favor, ayúdame*—oh God, please

help me!" I say, doing the trinity sign across my chest, then kissing my Confirmation picture. I look really hard at Abuela's smiling face.

"Chanel, you better get out here!" Mom yells again.

Taking a deep breath, I walk out of my bedroom. My knees are shaking more than the Tin Man's in *The Wizard of Oz*.

If looks could kill, I would be dead, judging by the pained expression on my mother's face. Her dark brown eyes are breathing fire. She is wearing black leotards and tights, and she is sweating because she has been exercising.

"That was the credit card company on the phone. They were calling me because of the excessive charges made on *my* credit card. But I don't have to tell *you* who's been making them, do I?" Mom challenges me.

"No, *Mamí*," I whimper. I know I am *finito*. It is time for my last rites, and I wish Father Nuñez was here to read them.

"Why did you do it, when I told you not to?" Mom screams. "I give you an inch, and you take a mile. *Por qué*, Chanel? Why? *Por qué?*"

I start crying. I feel like such an idiot for thinking I could get away with charging all that stuff on my mom's credit card. "I don't know why I did it," I stutter. "I was just mad at you."

"*You* were mad at *me*?" she says, turning up the volume another notch. "Are you kidding me? I give you my credit card—I trust you—and you're mad at me?"

"You won't let me be close to Pamela," I complain, letting it all hang out. I figure at this point, *que será, será*, as they say in the old movie. What will be, will be. "She's not a *bruja*, like you always call her. She's nice. She's nicer to me than you!" I'm really crying now, and so is my mom. I don't know who is angrier at who.

"Oh, yeah? Maybe you'd like her for a mother instead of me?" she says, half sobbing. "I let you buy a new outfit, and this is how you repay me?"

"At least Pamela wouldn't complain about me being in the Cheetah Girls!" I say, really letting the hot sauce fly. "You don't want me to go after my dreams—you only want me to give up on them, like you did!" Years ago, Mom gave up on being a model when she got to "a certain age." I know what I'm saying is unfair and mean, but I'm so mad now that I just can't stop myself.

The Cheetah Girls

"I want you to get out of my face until I talk to your father about this, but don't think for one second you're gonna get away with it!" Mom screams. "You can forget about all your stupid Cheetah Girls, too. *Tu entiendes?* You understand?"

No way. She can't do that! The Cheetah Girls is all I care about besides Abuela and my dad and Princess Pamela and Pucci and *arroz con pollo* and Prada! The Cheetah Girls and my dreams to travel all over the world are my whole life! Without them, I have *nada. La odia mi mami!* I hate my mother.

"I have to go to Drin-ka-ka Conservatory," I say, so nervous I can't even get the words out. "I promised everyone I'd be there."

"All right. You can go to this one last class," she says. "But you come right back afterward and wait for me here. *Entiendes?*"

"*Sí*," I whimper, then grab my jacket and run out the door.

After vocal class, I am slobbering like a baby to my crew.

Bubbles is so mad at me, she won't even talk to me. "You have broken a sacred rule of the

Cheetah Girls, Chuchie, and I am so disgusted with you, I cannot even look at you," she yells in front of Angie, Aqua, and Do' Re Mi.

I do not know what sacred rule Bubbles is talking about, but I am sure she will tell me, and anyway, I'm too afraid to ask. Drinka, who runs the conservatory, has left us alone in the rehearsal space, because big mouth Bubbles has told her what happened. We are sitting on the hardwood floor in a circle.

"How come you didn't tell me what you were doing with that credit card, Chuchie? You were always so sneaky-deaky, even when we were little!" Bubbles blurts out. She won't stop.

"Is your mother really gonna make you leave the group?" Do' Re Mi asks me, looking worried and scared.

"I don't know. That's what she says!" I cry. I am so scared of going home. I want Bubbles to help me. She's always helped me when I get in trouble, ever since we were little.

"I have no idea why Aunt Juanita wants you to be a buyer. You would end up wearing all the clothes yourself! Like I said before, you're a shopaholic waiting to happen!" Bubbles yells at me.

"Dag, now you've *really* given your mother a good reason not to let you stay in the group," Angie clucks, looking down at her skirt, then pulling it past her knees.

"Yeah, and now she's gonna say that *we* are a bad influence on you. You better let her know we didn't have anything to do with this—and you can take back all those clothes you bought me. I don't want them!" Do' Re Mi yells at me. Her eyes are watering.

Dorinda is a big crybaby. I know because she calls me on the phone and tells me secrets that Bubbles doesn't even know about. Like the stuff about her first foster mother, who was really mean to her and gave Dorinda up, but kept her sister. That's how she got put in Mrs. Bosco's house when she was almost five years old.

"Chuchie, the Cheetah Girls are all we have," Bubbles says. "We are not like some other stupid group. We don't just sing. We are more than just some singing group, okay?" She waves her hand at me, rolls her eyes, and pulls out her cell phone. "Let me call my mom at her shop. Auntie Juanita will be there, too, Chuchie, and my mom will know what to do."

I cover my face with my hands. I just want this bad dream to go away. Everybody is real quiet while Bubbles talks to her mom on the phone.

"Keep Juanita there, Mom. *Please* help us. Think of something!" Bubbles pleads to my *madrina* on the phone.

She listens for a minute, then says to me, "Mom says get your compact out and powder your nose." I know that this is *madrina*'s way of saying "sit tight and get ready for Freddy, 'cuz anything could go down."

"Juanita is still in the store screaming, so Mom is gonna call me back," Bubbles explains to all of us. "She's gonna calm Juanita down and think of what to do. And you know my mom can think on her feet, even if she's wearing shoes with ten-inch heels that are too tight," she adds, flossing.

"I know that's right," quips Aqua.

Dorothea is no joke. She can wheel and deal and, hopefully, she will save me from being the subject of a missing person's report.

"You're gonna pay for this one, Chuchie. In full," Bubbles says, putting away the cell phone. "Your mom is *caliente* mad!"

Angie hands me a pack of tissues out of her backpack. I take one and hand it back to her. "No, keep the whole thing, 'cuz you're gonna need 'em by the time your mother gets through with you," Angie clucks, then unzips her backpack and takes out a sandwich. "I'm sorry, y'all, but I'm hungry. We didn't have time to eat breakfast."

"I hope you're burning a good-luck money candle, Chuchie, because you're going to need all the luck you can get," Bubbles says, rolling her eyes at me. "Even though those candles look like a bunch of green wax to me, I don't see any duckets dropping from the sky to save you right now!"

It's a good thing Bubbles's cell phone rings, because I want to crown her like a queen for being so mean to me. Bubbles pulls up the phone antenna and hops on her Miss Wiggy StarWac Phone like it is a Batphone or something. Then she says, "Hmm, hmm," all serious—at least ten times, and keeps us waiting in suspense like a soap opera. My godmother is obviously giving her the *super ataque*, the blow-by-blow report.

When Bubbles hangs up, she lets out a sigh.

"You are so lucky, Chuchie," she says, pulling one of my braids. Then she gives us a blow-by-blow of the soap opera that is filming at Toto in New York . . . Fun in Diva Sizes, *madrina*'s boutique in Soho.

"Chuchie, your mom came into the store screaming so loud that Toto ran into the dressing room and scared a poor customer who was getting undressed," Bubbles explains.

The twins laugh, but I don't. Neither do Bubbles nor Dorinda. "We have to go to the boutique right now. *All* of us," Galleria says.

We all look at each other and swallow hard. It's high noon. Time for the big showdown. Ready or not, here we come!

Chapter 7

Dorothea is yelling at a man outside the boutique when we get there. Toto in New York . . . Fun in Diva Sizes is a *muy famoso* boutique, and many famous divas shop there, including Jellybean Nyce, the Divas, Sista Fudge, Queen Latifah, and even Starbaby, the newscaster who wears so much gold you have to wear sunglasses when you watch her on television. Dorothea does not play hide-and-seek with all the riffraff that comes to Soho looking to pickpocket all the tourists.

"You see what the sign says? It says, 'Toto in New York . . . Fun In Diva Sizes,'" Dorothea says with her hands on her hips, drilling the man, whose clothes look rumpled and crumpled. "This is a clothing store, not a toothless-men-who-love-big-women dating service, so get outta here!"

The man grins at Dorothea, then smacks his lips like he hasn't eaten *lonchando*. Then he hobbles away with his bottle in his hand, babbling like a parrot.

"He doesn't have any teeth," I mumble to Bubbles.

Because the door of the store is wide open, Toto comes running out. He is probably still afraid because of all the commotion. He looks so cute and fierce in the little cheetah-print suit Bubbles made for him, and he's as fierce as a cheetah, too! He jumps on the back of the legs of the man who has never had a visit from a tooth fairy.

"Toto, come here! Don't go running after him like he has treats for you!" Bubbles yells, then grabs Toto and carries him back inside the store, rubbing his stomach. Toto likes to get attention from anybody.

"Hi, Toto," I say, giving him a rub, too. I love him so much. I guess I'll never get a dog of my own now, though. . . .

"Dag, it must be hard having a store in New York, because there are a lot of crazy people here," Angie says.

There are a lot of people in New York who are cuckoo, but maybe not as "loco as Coco," I think, feeling sorry for myself. I climb up the stairs and inside the store, like a prisoner going to the electric chair. There is my mom, sitting on a stool with her arms crossed in front of her, and her eyes shooting bullets at me.

Luckily, my *madrina* takes over the situation, as usual, as soon as I get inside. "Chanel, I'm going to lay out the situation for you like the latest design collection. Juanita doesn't want you to be in the group anymore. And in many ways I don't think you deserve to be," my *madrina* says.

Now both my mom *and* my *madrina*, who I love so much, are ganging up on me! I haven't eaten anything all day, and I feel really dizzy, but I don't say anything. I just stand there.

Dorothea, wearing a dalmatian-dotted caftan, has her hands on her hips and is looking at my mom but standing over me, which makes me feel smaller than Dorinda. I know I'm not going to be a Cheetah Girl anymore. I'm so sad, I burst into tears.

"Now, I don't think that making you leave the group is going to teach you anything,

Chanel, and I know how much this means to Galleria, so we've worked out a solution," Dorothea continues. "You are going to work part-time in my store and pay back every penny you charged up on Juanita's cards, even if it takes you till you're a very old Cheetah Girl!"

Gracias, Dios! I say to myself. Thank goodness! My prayers have been answered! I don't have to leave the Cheetah Girls after all!

"Thank you, Dorothea! Thank you, *Mamí!*" I gush, the tears streaming down my face. "I will pay back all the money, *te juro*—I swear! And thank you sooo much for letting me stay in the group!"

All the other girls let out a shout of sheer relief, and hug me tight. But a word from my *madrina* makes them quiet down.

"We're not finished with you yet, *señorita*," Dorothea says, looking at me and getting more serious. "You know, Chanel, we all love to shop. It's fun, but it is not something you do when you are unhappy, or mad at someone, or looking for *love*, or for approval from kids in school. Love you get from your family, your friends—your mom—not Oophelia's catalog. If you are shopping with money you don't have—whether you are a child or a grown-up—then you have a problem, and you've got to own up to it, and change your ways."

Even though I don't say anything, I nod my head so Dorothea and my mom know that I understand.

"Mom, I like that," Bubbles says all excitedly, then whips out her notebook.

"Like what, darling?" Dorothea says, not at all amused.

"What you said about shopping for love. I'm going to write a song about this!"

"That's nice, darling, just don't act like you're large and in charge with *my* credit card."

"Yes, Mom," Bubbles says meekly.

"Mrs. Simmons, I wanna give back the outfit Chanel bought me. Is that okay?" Do' Re Mi asks quietly.

"No, Dorinda, you keep that. Chanel is gonna pay for it, so you might as well wear it," Mom says.

Nobody is stupider than I am, I think to myself. Why couldn't I be smart like Bubbles, or Dorinda? "When do I start working?" I ask.

"There's no time like the present," Dorothea

quips, then looks at Bubbles and the rest of our crew.

"I got a Spanish quiz tomorrow, so I'd better study," Bubbles says, then picks up Toto and gives him a kiss on his nose. "Bye, Boo-boo— you be a good boy, and help Mom chase away all the bozos!"

"Knowing Toto, I'm surprised he didn't ask that man for a sip of wine from that bottle he was carrying!" Dorothea says, opening up the cash register.

Do' Re Mi picks up her backpack and puts it on her munchkin shoulders, saying, "Guess he's just tippin' when he's not sippin'!" She is making a joke on the Drinka Champagne's disco song from back in the day. I can see we're all feeling a lot better—most of all, me! Good old Dorothea—she is the best!

"It's gonna be all right," she tells my mom. "Don't write Miss Cuchifrito off yet. She isn't crazy, just lazy, but she'll learn that duckets don't drop from the sky. Trust me."

They both laugh. It's the first time I've seen Mom smile since we got here. But then, Dorothea could make anybody laugh. She is *tan coolio.*

"Come here, baby," my mom says. I do, and she throws her arms around me. I hug her tight. "You know I love you so much. I've just got to be able to trust you, that's all."

"You can, *Mamí*," I tell her, meaning it with all my heart. "I'm gonna play it straight with you from now on." I hug her back, really tight. "And thanks for letting me stay in the Cheetah Girls."

"I know how much it means to you, baby," she tells me, as Dorothea and my crew look on, smiling. "After all, I've had dreams, too."

She and Dorothea smile at one another, and just for a second, I can imagine them when they were our age. Young, full of dreams, and chasing *la gran fantasía*.

"I love you, too, *Mamí*," I whisper, smiling and crying at the same time. "And from now on, you can trust me one hundred percent!"

"That's my Miss Cuchifrito!" Dorothea says, smiling. And we all share a laugh together.

Chapter 8

Mr. Johnson called us with good news this morning. Not only has he booked us, the Cheetah Girls, for the Amateur Hour contest at the world-famous Apollo Theatre on 125th Street, but he has talked Hal Hyena, the president of Hyena Records, into coming to see us perform!

"He says he called in a favor—'cuz we got the flava!" Bubbles types to me on the computer screen.

The Phat Planet chat room on the Internet has become my hangout, because, as Pucci so loudly announces to everybody, "*Loco Coco* is grounded!" But Aqua's idea about forming the Cheetah Girls Council and having meetings sure comes in "handy dandy" for a grounded *señorita* like myself.

I only get to go out to go to school, to work at Dorothea's boutique, and take classes at Drinka's. So, of course, our meetings have to be on-line, but that's okay. They really help.

I am not sad anymore about what happened, because I've learned a good lesson. I'm only sorry that I caused everybody so much trouble. I like working at the store, of course, because I love Dorothea. And slowly but surely, I'm paying back the money I owe my mom. Of course, at the rate I'm going, it's gonna take me about a year, but like they say, I made my bed, now I've gotta lie down in it.

"Loco Coco is grounded, *Papí*!" I can hear Pucci on the phone with my dad in the kitchen, which is way down the hall from my bedroom.

I'm finally going to see my dad tonight, and I'm going to tell him everything. I know he must have heard the whole story by now, though, and I'm sure I'm going to get yelled at big time.

"Do me a flava. Who's gonna come with me to see my dad?" I type on the screen.

"I want y'all to hear the lyrics I wrote for this

song," Bubbles types, ignoring my request. "Guess what the title is?"

"'You Think You Large 'Cuz You Charge'?" Do' Re Mi snaps.

"Cute, but no loot, Do' Re Mi! Anybody else want to take a crack at my new song attack?"

I have a title idea, so I type it in: "'Chanel Ain't So Swell'?"

"That was true when you broke one of our sacred commandments, but now it isn't, because you're working for the 'Benjamins.' Give up yet?"

"What's the sacred commandment, anyway?" Do' Re Mi types.

At least somebody had the nerve to ask.

"Um, let's see," Bubbles types in. I can just see her making up a snap on her feet. "'You can only do so much fibbing to your friends who've seen you in your spotted pj's before you're so far backed up in a corner, you come out boxing like a cuckoo kangaroo'? How's that?"

"Galleria, you're a mess!!!!" Angie types in. "But that is the truth you're preaching, because the Lord don't like lies."

"Or flies!" Do' Re Mi types in.

Oh, just what I need—for the gospel hour to begin. When Aqua and Angie get started, you never know when it's going to end.

Bubbles isn't having it, though. "Okay, back to name that tune? Y'all give up yet?"

"Yes!" we all type one by one.

"It's called, 'Shop in the Name of Love,'" Bubbles types.

Leave it to Bubbles. Nobody is better with words than she is.

"Come on, Bubbles, let's see the Cheetah-licious lyrics!"

"Not now, brown cows. I want Mr. Johnson to hear it first when we go to the studio again. Maybe he and Pumpmaster Pooch will let us record it for our demo tape!"

"What time do we have to be at the studio?" Do' Re Mi asks. "Mrs. Bosco has got to go down to the agency with Twinkie, another one of her foster kids, so I'm on baby-sitting duty."

"We have to be there by ten o'clock," Angie responds.

Basta. Enough. I need help here, and nobody's paying any attention. "Listen, I feel like a *holograma* because no one is answering me! I have to go my dad's store tonight—who's gonna come with me?" I type, hoping Bubbles will take the steak bait. She loves my dad's Shake-a-Steak sandwich.

"We'll go with you," Angie types.

"I'll come, too, but I gotta drop Toto off to Dr. Bowser, the doggie dentist, first," Bubbles types.

"Maybe if you didn't give him so much Double Dutch Rocco Choco ice cream he wouldn't have to go to the dentist," I type. I mean, Toto eats too many treats.

"I'm gonna let you slide the read ride this time, Chuchie, since you are seriously grounded, but we'll be there to back you up," says Bubbles.

"*Está bien!*" I type back. That's my crew for you. Always down for the 'do. And not just hairdos either.

We are really pouting on the way to my dad's store. It's a good thing we've still got Amateur Hour at the Apollo Theatre coming up, because our session at the studio did not go well at all. If the song Pumpmaster Pooch and Mr. Johnson had us singing the first time was *la wacka*, you had to hear the one he gave us the second time around.

"It was called 'Can I Get a Burp?'" Bubbles

moaned as soon as she read the title. "What are we now, cows? she asked. "I don't think these guys get our image, and I'm not going out like that. Did you hear how they responded to my 'Shop in the Name of Love' lyrics?"

"Word, I noticed it. When you showed him the song, he looked at you like you were a stray dog or something," Do' Re Mi says.

"Let's sing some of it together before we go in to Killer Tacos, yo?" Bubbles says, looking at us.

"We're always down for the singing swirl, Bubbles!" Do' Re Mi says, leading us on as we start to sing "Shop in the Name of Love."

"Honey may come from bees
but money don't grow on trees.
When you shop in the name of love
you gotta ask yourself
What are you dreamin' of?
What are you schemin' of?
What are you trippin' on, love?"

By the time we get to the refrain, we are on 96th Street and Broadway, two steps from my dad's store. Then we do the cute "call and response" refrain that comes at the end of the song. We're groovin' from all the people watching us sing.

> *"Polo or solo.*
> *Say what?*
> *I want Gucci or Pucci.*
> *Say what?*
> *It's Prada or nada.*
> *Yeah—you got that?*
> *Uh-huh, I got that.*
> *Excuse me, Miss, does that dress come in red or blue?*
> *Oh, no?*
> *Well, that's alright 'cuz the cheetah print will always do!*
> *The Cheetah Girls are large and in charge*
> *but that don't mean that we charge up our cards!*
> *The Cheetah Girls are large and in charge*
> *but that don't mean we charge up our cards!"*

We finish with a big dance flourish, and all of a sudden, people all around us on the street are applauding, whooping it up, and shouting for more!

"I don't care how many pound cake remixes

Pumpmaster Pooch did for Sista Fudge, nobody writes *más coolio* songs than my Bubbles," I exclaim.

"Yeah, but how are we gonna get in a studio and do the songs *we* love?" Do' Re Mi adds, hitching up her backpack.

"Yeah, 'cuz we sure don't have songs-we-love money for no studio time," Bubbles says sadly.

"Maybe I could ask Princess Pamela," I say excitedly.

"Sure, Chuchie, as if you aren't in enough trouble for two lifetimes!" Bubbles says, then pulls my braids. "Excuse me, does that dress come in red or blue?"

We are laughing, right up until we see my father standing by the door. He is obviously waiting just for us, and I can tell he is grass-hopping mad.

"*Ay, Dios mío*, Chuchie, his eyes are breathing fire hotter than his Dodo Mojo Salsa Picante," Bubbles says, trying to make a joke. Nobody laughs, though. We all get real quiet.

"Hi, *Papí*," I say, squeaking. I have a little knot in my stomach, even though I want to hug him. I decide not to say one more word. I'm in enough *agua caliente*—hot water—as it is.

Then I see the anger go right out of his eyes. He takes a handkerchief out of his pocket and wipes his forehead. "You girls are late. I was getting worried. I don't like you walking around the city at night, *tú entiendes?*"

"*Sí,*" I say softly.

He takes us inside, and we sit down in one of the red plastic booths. Both he and Princess Pamela have red chairs in their stores—hers are velvet, though. Dad looks right at me. His eyes look very sad. Then he reaches into his pocket, takes out my copy of Mr. Johnson's agreement, and lays it on the table.

"Now, listen," he says, lowering his voice. "I don't have an opinion one way or the other. But I just got off the phone with Pamela, and she says you girls shouldn't sign this agreement."

"Why doesn't she want us to sign?" I ask.

"You mean because she got a psychic feeling, or something?" Do' Re Mi asks.

"Yes, I guess that's what you could call it," he says, pulling on his salt-and-pepper goatee. "But if I know one thing about Pamela, her premonitions are not to be played with, *entiendes?*"

We all look at each other like we've just seen a monster.

"Pamela said, 'Tell the Cheetah Girls to stay away from the animals.' She said Chanel would understand," my dad explains, looking at me again.

"What animals?" I respond, acting all innocent, nervous that the spotlight is now on me. I realize she must have known it was me on the phone all those times. How embarrassing!

All of a sudden, *la lucha*—the light—goes on inside my head, and I see what Princess Pamela was trying to tell me over the phone. "Beware of predators who run in packs," I remember her saying to me. "They will prey on your good fortune. They will circle around you like vultures and steal what is yours."

It wasn't the Cheetah Girls she was trying to warn me about! "Oh, snapples—Mr. Jackal Johnson and Mr. Hyena!" I gasp. "Jackals and Hyenas. *Those* are the animals!"

"What should we do?" Angie asks, nibbling on one of her Pee Wee Press-On Nails, then tapping her hand on the table nervously. "I mean, it's only a premonition . . . and we've got this big gig comin' up at the Apollo. . . ."

"Let me see what my mom thinks," Bubbles says, acting large and in charge, and taking her cell phone out of her backpack. These days, we are depending on Dorothea *más y más*—more and more.

"My mom can't see the future, but she can smell an okeydokey from the OK corral a mile away!" Bubbles quips. Over the phone, she explains the situation to her mom.

When she hangs up, Bubbles has a satisfied smile on her face. She says, "Mom says she has a call in to Mrs. Eagle, her lawyer, to see what she thought about the agreement. She'll let us know as soon as she gets a peep."

"So," Dad says, turning to me like a secret agent. "Did you at least *win* that Prada bag?"

"Nope," I say, looking sheepish, because my dad obviously knows everything, thanks to the Mummy, aka my mom. "Can you believe Derek Hambone did—and he only bought one ticket!"

Shaking his head, Dad asks, "What about that date with Krusher?"

Ay, Dios! He really does know everything.

"Nope," I say, all sad, so at least my dad will feel sorry for me. "Can you believe some DJ from WLIB radio won? It's so unfair!"

All of a sudden, Dad lets out a roar of a

laugh, showing his big, big teeth. "That contest must've been rigged!"

"And you *know* Chuchie made more calls to that 900 number than the rest of us make in a year!" Do' Re Mi says.

We all laugh. Then me and my dad do something we haven't done in a long time. We hug each other real tight, and I start crying. "I love you, *Papí*."

"I know, *mía princesa*," he says, stroking my head as I lean against his shoulder. "I love you, too—but you really can't 'shop in the name of love.'"

I look at my dad in surprise.

"I heard you girls singing outside," Dad says, raising his thick eyebrows. "A deaf man could hear you down the block. I think Pamela is right, though—the Cheetah Girls are gonna make a lot of people happy—especially *my* Cheetah Girl!"

Chapter 9

I am humming to myself on the way out my front door, when I stub my toe really hard on a case of Pucci's Burpy's soda that is sitting in the hallway. "Pucci, could you put this box in the kitchen, *por favor*!" I yell out. "It's in the way! I just tripped right over it!"

"I don't care, just do it yourself!" Pucci says, running into his room. He has been mad at me all day because I got to see Dad and he didn't.

"You know, for all that money I spent on ballet lessons for you, you are *clumsy*," Mom yells at me from the kitchen. She is wearing a turban on her head with a big diamond broach in the middle, and is all dressed up to go meet Mr. Tycoon at the airport.

"Mom, how come Pucci gets to order Burpy's soda from the Internet?" I yell back at her.

"Your ordering days are over till you can buy it yourself, that's why!" she says.

"Mom, I'm going to the meeting at Mr. Johnson's," I say. Bubbles's mom has called the meeting, but she won't say why. Only that her lawyer called her back, and she wants to straighten things out with Mr. Johnson. I'm worried about it—I know Princess Pamela warned us about him, but he's the only manager we've got—and we've got our demo coming out, and the gig at the Apollo—if it doesn't work out with Mr. Johnson, what are we gonna do?

All Mom says is "Be back in time for dinner, Chanel. And tell Dorothea the Dolce & Gabbana sample sale starts at ten o'clock tomorrow."

"*Está bien.*" Too bad I won't be going to the sample sale, I think to myself as I close the door. But these days, and until I pay off what I owe my mom, shopping and me are total strangers.

Everyone is quiet when I walk into Mr. Johnson's office, and they all turn to look at me.

They must be early, because I know I'm not late, I think. Nervously, I look at my Miss Wiggy! watch.

"Let's cut to the paper chase here, Mr. Johnson. This contract is not going to work," Dorothea says, looking up from her leopard brim and right into Mr. Johnson's eyes.

"Mrs. Garibaldi, I can assure you this contract is pretty standard," Mr. Johnson says, smoothing down his bright red tie. "We're only talking about production costs."

"According to my lawyer, at the royalty rate you have written in this clause, the only game the Cheetah Girls are gonna be able to afford for the next ten years is jumping jacks!" Dorothea snaps at Mr. Johnson, then leans over his desk.

Bubbles looks at me and puts her finger over her mouth. I can see that I have walked right into another soap opera.

"I am footing the cost of the demo tape, wheeling and dealing to make everything happen for the Cheetah Girls, so it's only fitting that *I'm* sitting on the throne and seeing my girls become stars," Mr. Johnson says, slamming his hands down on his desk.

"You're going to be seeing 'stars,' all right—right after I clunk you with my purse!" Dorothea says, her dark brown eyes getting squinty. "You are no longer going to manage *my* girls. And, if you ever come sniffing around them again, Mr. *Jackal*, or if you try to release any of those songs with their vocals on it, I'm gonna come back and be so shady the sun is gonna go down on you. Do you understand?" Dorothea says in that scary voice she gets when she is mad. Leave it to my *madrina* to throw her weight around and show who is the conductor on this choo-choo train.

"What about the girls' gig at the Apollo? I hooked it up so Mr. Hyena can be there. I mean, I'm digging your concern, Mrs. Garibaldi, but I think you're making a big mistake," Mr. Johnson says, swiveling in his fake leather chair. There are little beads of sweat on his forehead, like I get when I'm scared.

"The only mistake I'm making is that I don't hit you over the head with my pocketbook, you hungry scavenger!" Dorothea says, then motions for us to get up with her.

We all walk out of the office behind

Dorothea, and big-mouthed Bubbles says to Mr. Johnson, "See ya around like a doughnut!"

Why can't I think of the kinds of things that Bubbles says? I start smiling and looking at my crew, but Angie and Aqua look sad.

"It would have been nice to perform at the Apollo. What are we gonna do now?" Aqua says, popping her gum.

"Don't pop gum in public, darling, you're too pretty for that," Dorothea says, then puts her arm around Aqua.

"I'm sorry, Mrs.—I mean *Ms.* Dorothea. I was just kinda nervous in there," Aqua explains. She puts the pink blob of gum in a tissue and throws it in the garbage receptacle by the elevator.

"Now we don't have a demo tape. We don't have a show. We don't have nothing. What *are* we gonna do, Ms. Dorothea?" Angie says, crossing her arms and pouting like a Texas Tornado cheerleader.

"Maybe we missed our last chance, last dance. Was the contract really that bad, Ms. Dorothea?" Do' Re Mi asks, looking up at my *madrina*, who is more than a foot taller than her, especially with her high heels on. They are bright-red patent-leather pumps that look good enough to eat.

Eat? Suddenly, I realize that I'm hungry.

"Some Dominican-style *arroz con pollo* would be great right about now," I say to Bubbles.

"Darlings, I know this fabulous Moroccan restaurant we can go to around the corner. My treat!" Dorothea says, pulling out her compact. "Listen, Cheetah Girls, don't get so nervous you're ready to pounce at the first opportunity that comes along. We're gonna figure out something, okay? It takes more than one shifty jackal to chase us out of the jiggy jungle, am I right?"

Dorothea looks at us, extends her hands, and does the Cheetah Girls handshake with all five of us.

"You got that right, Momsy poo—we are gonna do what we gotta do!" Bubbles says, egging her on. "Even if we did miss the opportunity of a lifetime, and even if it takes us longer, we're still gonna get diggity, no doubt. It's just a matter of time."

"I hear that," Do' Re Mi says, then sighs. She's trying to keep her spirits up—we all are—but it's hard not to keep thinking about everything we've just lost.

Because we are so down in *la dumpa*, after our *lonchando*, Dorothea asks us to come to her store so she can give us a surprise. When we get to the store, my mom is there! I wonder what's going on.

"What are you doing here, Auntie Juanita?" Bubbles asks my mom. I'm thinking, I hope Mr. Tycoon's plane didn't get hijacked! Mom puts her sunglasses on her head, and holds up a newspaper. It's the latest issue of the *Uptown Express*. "Did you see this?" she says, handing Dorothea the newspaper.

"Hmmph, the hyenas are circling after all!" Dorothea says, showing it to us. "Hyena Records Sings Its Last Note, And Its Founder Is Singing Like a Crow to the Feds!" We all gather around the newspaper, as Dorothea reads us the article blow by blow.

"Seems that Mr. Johnson and Mr. Hyena were in cahoots all along," Dorothea explains.

"What's a cahoot?" Angie asks.

"That means they were the okeydokey duo,

get it?" Bubbles says. "They were flipping the flimflam together."

"Oh," Angie says, shaking her head. "They weren't doing right by us. I get it."

"Angie, they were crooks!" Do' Re Mi blurts out, then plops down on Dorothea's leopard love seat.

"Seems Mr. Johnson would steer artists to the record label," Dorothea says.

Before she can continue, Bubbles blurts out, "Signing them to these *radickio* deals, like the one he was trying to perpetrate on us!"

"That's right, darling," Dorothea says, reaching for one of the Godiva chocolates on the counter. "Then Mr. Hyena would cover the royalty tracks, so that the artists never knew how much they were making, and the two would skim the profits out of the company."

"So Princess Pamela was right after all!" I blurt out, then realize that I should buy some Krazy Glue and stick my lips together permanently.

My mom looks at me like she is already picking out the color of my coffin.

"Juanita, I'm gonna side with Chanel on this one," Dorothea says, putting her arm around my mom as she explains Princess Pamela's predictions to her. "She may not be your cup of tea, but she sure knows how to read tea leaves!" Dorothea says, doing the Cheetah Girls handshake with us.

Mom thinks for a minute, her face all serious. "I don't mind if you see her," she says to me all of sudden. "You just cannot take any presents from her, or call her Psychic Hot Line—I don't care if she invented the crystal ball!"

"I told you, *Mamí*, I won't take anything from her again," I say nervously.

"You know what mothers are?" Mom asks me.

"What?"

"Psychics who don't charge—you can get all the advice you need for *free!*" My mom smiles, slapping Dorothea a high five.

"Well, I'm glad you all are happy—but we still don't have a demo," Aqua says, reaching into the box of Godiva. She must be getting very comfortable around here, because she used to always ask Dorothea first.

"Help yourself, darling," Dorothea says.

"Oh, I'm sorry, Ms. Dorothea!" Aqua blurts out.

"That's all right, just enjoy yourself," Dorothea says, smiling.

"Chanel, are you sure those Chihuahuas don't shed hair?" Mom asks me.

"I'm very sure, because Do' Re Mi looked it up in a book!" I say.

"That's right, Mrs. Simmons, I did," Do' Re Mi says, helping me out.

"Maybe next weekend, we'll see if we find one for Pucci's birthday," Mom says.

I can't believe my ears. "Oh, *Mamí*," I say, and run over to hug her.

"Don't hug me yet. If he sheds one hair, he's going right back to the dog pound," Juanita quips.

"Why do you have to get a 'he'?" Do' Re Mi quips.

"Because Pucci hates girls—except for Bubbles," I volunteer with a giggle, then sit Toto in my lap. "He's not like you, Boo-boo, right?"

Ms. Dorothea motions for all of us to sit down. "Now, the reason why I wanted all of you to come back to the store . . ." She breaks out in a big smile. "I have a little surprise for you, Cheetah Girls." Dorothea brushes her wavy wiglet hairs out of her face. "Remember I told you Jellybean Nyce was in here shopping?"

"Really!" Angie says. "OmiGod, we love her!"

"I know. And I told her about your predicament, and she is gonna hook us up with the producer who did *her* demo, Chili Dog Watkins."

"*Really*?" Bubbles blurts out.

"Really," Dorothea counters. "But I'm not finished. I, Dorothea Garibaldi, have secured the fabulous Cheetah Girls a spot on The Amateur Hour at the world-famous Apollo!"

"No way, Jose!" I say, my mouth hanging open. "How did you do that, *madrina*?"

"I did it the way *every* manager does—I sold you like the second coming of the Spice Rack Girls, that's how," Dorothea brags. "You'll never say I don't work overtime for *my* artists."

"Mom, are you saying what I think you're saying?" Bubbles asks, smiling and putting her arm around Dorothea.

"Darling, one can never be too sure what you're thinking, but I'll tell you what I'm saying," Dorothea says, looking at all of us. "It's time for the Cheetah Girls to have *real* management—and you're looking at her."

We scream with delight, while Mom just looks on from the counter, amused. "I hope you know what you're doing, Dottie, because these girls will wear you out!"

"Oh, I know what I'm doing. I'm taking the Cheetah Girls right to the top, where they belong."

Angie can't contain her Southern charm any longer, and screams out, "Come on Mr. Sandman, show me your hook, 'cuz I'm ready for Freddy!"

Angie, of course, is referring to the famous bozo with the hook who runs bad acts off the stage if they get booed by the audience. The Sandman kinda looks like a brown clown, but his antics are no joke, for sure.

"All I can say is, I hope Freddy is ready for us at the world-famous Apollo," Bubbles adds.

All I can say is, *la dopa!*

"Come on, Cheetah Girls," Bubbles shouts. "Let's give the world a taste of our latest, greatest hit!"

We break into "Shop in the Name of Love," and the whole place is rockin', customers and all. We look at each other and smile, nodding our heads. Me most of all, 'cuz I'm so glad this all happened. It was all worth it, all the grief, all the tears—just to come out of it with a song like this one.

Yeah—it's just a matter of time. Look out, world—the Cheetah Girls are comin'—and we are large and in charge!

Shop in the Name of Love

Polo or solo
Gucci or Pucci
Prada or Nada
is the way I wanna live

Ma don't make me wait
or I'll gaspitate
till I get my own credit card
and sashay right to the bargain yard!

That's right, y'all
Honey may come from bees
but money don't grow on trees.
You may think you're large
'cuz you charge
But you're looking good
and sleeping on a barge!

When you shop in the Name Of Love
you gotta ask yourself
What are you dreamin' of?

What are you schemin' of?
What are you trippin' on, love?

That's right, y'all!
The Cheetah Girls are large
and in charge
but that don't mean
we charge up our cards

The Cheetah Girls are large
and in charge
but that don't mean
we charge up our cards

Polo or solo
Gucci for Pucci
Prada or nada
is the way I wanna live

Say what?

Polo or solo
Gucci for Pucci
Prada or nada
is the way I wanna live

You got that?
Yeah. I got that.
Excuse, Miss,
does that dress come in red or blue?
Well, that's allright
'cuz the cheetah print
will always do!

The Cheetah Girls are large
and in charge
but that don't mean
we charge up our cards
You got that?
Yeah. I got that!

That's right, y'all
Honey may come from bees
but money don't grow on trees.
You may think you're large
'cuz you charge
But you're looking good
and sleeping on a barge

When you shop in the Name of Love
you gotta ask yourself

What are you dreamin' of?
What are you schemin' of?
What are you trippin' on, love?

The Cheetah Girls are large
large and in charge
but that don't mean
we charge up our cards
You got that?
Yeah. I got that!

The Cheetah Girls Glossary

Abuela: Grandmother.

Adobo down: Mad flava.

Arroz con pollo: Rice and chicken.

Benjamins: Bucks, dollars.

Bruja: A good or bad witch.

Caliente mad: Really angry.

Confirmation: Catholic religion ceremony at the age of thirteen.

Cuatro yuks!: When something or someone is four times yucky.

Do me a flava: Do me a favor.

Down for the 'do: Ready to support.

Duckets: Money, loot.

Está bien: Awright.

Fib-eronis: Teeny-weeny fibs.

Flipping the flim-flam: Acting or doing something shady.

Floss: Show off.

Frijoles: Beans.

Gracias gooseness: Thank goodness.

La dopa!: Fabulous.

La gran fantasía: Living in Happyville.

La wacka: Something that is wack.

Lonchando: Lunching.

Madrina: Godmother.

Majordomo: Legitimate.

Mentira: A not-so-little lie.

Muy coolio: Very cool.

Piñata-whacking mad: When someone is madder than *caliente* mad.

Poco paz: A little peace.

Qué broma!: What a joke!

Querida: Dear. Precious one.

Radickio: Ridiculous!

Ready for Freddy: Ready to do your thing, no matter what happens.

Schemo: Idiot

Tan coolio: So cool.

Tú sabes que tú sabes: You know what you know.

Weakness for carats: Someone who is a lifetime member of the diamonds-are-a-girl's-best-friend club.

Wheel-a-deala: Making moves, both good or bad.

Winky dink: Blink and you'll miss it.

Yo tengo un coco: I have a crush!

ABOUT THE AUTHOR

Deborah Gregory earned her growl power as a diva-about-town contributing writer for ESSENCE, VIBE, and MORE magazines. She has showed her spots on several talk shows including OPRAH, RICKI LAKE, and MAURY POVICH. She lives in New York City with her pooch, Cappuccino, who is featured as the Cheetah Girls' mascot, Toto.

 JUMP AT THE SUN

Pounce on The Cheetah Girls' newest book!

Who's 'Bout to Bounce?

Dorinda is the dance diva of the Cheetah Girls. But when Dorinda's dance teacher tells her she's got what it takes to audition as a back-up dancer for singing sensation Mo' Money Monique, she knows that this could be her big break. But if she makes the cut, she'll have to leave the Cheetah Girls behind. Will Dorinda go out on her own or stay loyal to the group?

Coming to Bookstores November 1999.